PROVOKED

ENLIGHTENMENT TRILOGY - BOOK ONE

JOANNA CHAMBERS

JOANNA CHAMBERS
AUTHOR

Provoked

Copyright © 2017 Joanna Chambers

2nd edition

Cover art: Natasha Snow

Editor: Linda Ingmanson

Published by Joanna Chambers

ISBN: 9781548175634

❀ Created with Vellum

Provoked

Tormented by his forbidden desires for other men and the painful memories of the childhood friend he once loved, lawyer David Lauriston tries to maintain a celibate existence while he forges his reputation in Edinburgh's privileged legal world.

But then, into his repressed and orderly life, bursts Lord Murdo Balfour.

Cynical, hedonistic and utterly unapologetic, Murdo could not be less like David. And as appalled as David is by Murdo's unrepentant self-interest, he cannot resist the man's sway. Murdo tempts and provokes David in equal measure, forcing him to acknowledge his physical desires.

But Murdo is not the only man distracting David from his work. Euan MacLennan, the brother of a convicted radical David once represented, approaches David to beg him for help. Euan is searching for the government agent who sent his brother to Australia on a convict ship, and other radicals to the gallows. Despite knowing it may damage his career, David cannot turn Euan away.

As their search progresses, it begins to look as though the trail may lead to none other than Lord Murdo Balfour, and David has to wonder whether it's possible Murdo could be more than he seems. Is he really just a bored aristocrat, amusing himself at David's expense, or could he be the agent provocateur responsible for the fate of Peter MacLennan and the other radicals?

CHAPTER ONE

8th September 1820, Stirling, Scotland

The crowd for the executions of John Baird and Andrew Hardie had grown steadily all morning. When David had arrived to take up his place, he'd had room enough to stretch his arms wide. Now he was hemmed in on all sides, and by every kind of person—men, women and children, low- and high-born.

There were hundreds of supporters for the two men about to be hanged and beheaded, but there were plenty of people here for the sheer spectacle too. The general mood was that of any execution—a gently seething combination of morbid glee and bloodlust that could easily spill into violence but that, for now, had a holiday feel. All around, people pushed and shoved, seeking out the best views and shouting for their friends. Hawkers announced their wares in raucous voices as they elbowed their way through the throng, peddling hot pease and beans, sawster, oranges and gingerbread. The mingled sweet and savoury scents combined with the smell of too-close, unwashed bodies. David swallowed back a sudden urge to retch and wished he'd thought to bring a nip of whisky with him.

The redcoats were out in force—soldiers from the 13th Foot. They held back the rowdy rabble gathered on either side of Broad Street; two thin lines of scarlet coats, silver bayonets bristling. Behind them, a swarm of spectators jostled and heaved.

A sharp elbow caught David in the ribs, making him grunt. His aggressor was a woman in a dirty apron and cap who smelled strongly of drink. Evidently she wanted to be closer to the front, the better to see the brutal pageantry of it all. Once past David, she ploughed through a group of young men. They cursed her roundly, but she ignored them and blundered on.

David didn't grudge the woman her view. He hated executions. He was here because it was the only thing left that he could do for James and Andrew. He had tried his best to save them, but their trial had been a foregone conclusion. Flushed out into the open like hunted foxes, James and Andrew had sealed their fates months before, when they marched on Carron to take up arms and demand a say in who governed them. Little did they know that some of their number—the most committed and eager for the fight—were, in fact, hunting hounds sent by Whitehall. *Agents provocateurs.*

They never had a chance.

David shifted his feet, weary in body and soul. The last day and a half had been interminable. First the journey from Edinburgh, then the long hours at the inn, with nothing but his own thoughts for company. He'd come into town too early this morning, unsure how heavy the crowds would be. Already he'd been waiting more than two hours, stranded in a sea of people, some who looked as sick at heart as himself and others who might as well have been at the circus.

A sudden rumble at the top of the street caused the specta-tors to turn their heads as one.

"It's the procession!" a young woman ahead of David informed her neighbour excitedly. She wore a serving girl's apron and her fair curls peeped out from under her cap. She looked as wholesome as new-baked bread, and David couldn't imagine why she was here, rising up on her toes and craning her neck for a better look.

At first all David could see was a company of mounted dragoons, picking their way slowly down the hill from the castle, but as they drew nearer, he could just about make out the shape of a horse-drawn hurdle in their midst, carrying the condemned men.

It was the music, though, that reached him first, a full minute before the hurdle passed. A hymn. One his mother used to sing as she worked in the farm kitchen at home, *O God, Our Help in Ages Past*. The hymn moved with the procession as it progressed down the hill, each new segment of the crowd taking it up, bearing the prisoners along on uneven waves of song.

The hymn had an extraordinary effect. The hawkers' cries ceased and the excited spectators settled, until the only sounds breaking the silence were the clatter of the horses' hooves, the dragging rattle of the prisoners' hurdle on the cobblestones and this solemn choir of voices.

David sang too, his tenor voice a little hoarse, the familiar words dredged up from some long-forgotten corner of his memory.

Time, like an ever rolling stream
Bears all who breathe away,
They fly forgotten, as a dream
Dies at the opening day.

As the procession passed David, he caught a fleeting glimpse of the prisoners through a small gap between the mounted redcoats. They sat side by side on the hurdle, the headsman opposite them, a still, hooded figure, all in black.

Behind the hurdle and its military escort walked the local

dignitaries. The magistrates and Sheriff MacDonald himself, carrying his stave of office. As they moved onward, the calming effect of the hymn seemed to dissipate, and a few supporters of the condemned men bayed insults.

Once the procession had passed David, there was little to see for a while. The hurdle came to a halt outside the courthouse but there were so many redcoats bustling around that David saw nothing of the prisoners getting out. A woman in front of him reported that they had gone inside.

Long minutes passed, and the crowd grew impatient as it waited, regaining some of its dangerous mood. A few more spectators shoved past David to get closer to the scaffold for the main event, and David found himself being dragged along in their wake, ending up beside a group of men who looked as though they'd been drinking for some time.

They were dressed in worn, shabby clothes, and each carried a flagon of some ale or spirit. They made lewd jokes and deliberately jostled their neighbours, egging each other on. David tried to move away from them, but there were people at his back and on his right and left, all hard up against him. There was nowhere to go, so instead he averted his eyes and tried to ignore them.

A murmur of excitement went up as the courthouse doors opened again. From his new vantage point, David saw several figures emerge, and this time he was able to pick out the condemned men in their black clothes, their hands bound behind their backs. They looked amazingly calm as they walked over to the scaffold and began to mount the steps.

At this first sign of what was to come, the crowd rippled with expectation. A few cries went up. *Murder!* And *Shame!* Beside David, the drunken men laughed over a filthy story one was telling about the old whore he'd tupped the night before.

Once the prisoners were on the scaffold, James Baird

stepped forward to address the crowd. Although Baird's voice rang out, David could only hear snatches of his words.

"—die an ignominious death by unjust laws—"

A few exclamations of agreement at this.

"—be the means of our afflicted countrymen's speedy redemption—"

The men beside David kept talking, oblivious. Angry, he shot them a disapproving glance, and one of them noticed, a burly man with a pockmarked face. He gave David a long, ugly look and elbowed his neighbour to draw his attention. The second man listened to what the first had to say, his bleary, hostile gaze fixed on David.

David turned away, tamping down the sudden flare of rage that threatened to overcome the fear squatting in his gut. An urge to strike out—to just throw himself into a brawl he could never ever win—assailed him. He had to bite the inside of his cheek and tighten his fists till he thought his knuckles would split to get control of himself. He was here for one reason only: to witness James's and Andrew's deaths. To show them they would be remembered.

If Jeffrey knew David was here, he'd have a fit. He'd advised the younger man against taking the radicals' case at all, pointing out that it was one thing for Jeffrey to defend men who had taken up arms against the government, it was quite another for David Lauriston—the son of a tenant farmer from Fife with scarce four years as an advocate to his name—to join him. But David had taken the case anyway, realising his ambition to work with the great man. And it had brought him here today.

It was Hardie's turn to speak now, and he stepped forward. The first part of what he said was drowned out, but David heard his final words.

"—in a few minutes, our blood shall be shed on this scaffold," Hardie cried, "our heads severed from our bodies for no other sin than seeking the legitimate rights of our ill-used and downtrodden countrymen—"

Shouts of encouragement from the crowd echoed all around at his words. The sheriff surged forward to place a restraining hand on Hardie's arm.

"Stop this violent and improper language, Mr. Hardie!" he demanded. He was almost purple with anger. "You promised not to inflame the crowd!"

The spectators protested loudly at this silencing of the prisoner.

"Let him speak!" someone cried.

Hardie shrugged MacDonald's hand off, declaring angrily, "We said what we intended to say, whether you granted us liberty to do so or not."

A loud cheer greeted this, and it seemed to draw Hardie's attention to the throng of spectators. He looked about himself. Out at the crowd, then up at the gibbet above his head. At the block beside him, readied for his own beheading, then out at the crowd again. At the people grouped in the square to witness his death, all hemmed in by countless redcoats. Everywhere there was the scarlet of dress uniforms, the glint of weapons, the quiver of nervous horseflesh. David watched as the condemned man took it all in, and saw the potential of what might happen here today.

Hardie held up his hand and spoke one last time. "Do not drink any toasts to us tonight, friends." His voice rang out clearly, but his tone was sombre as he eyed the soldiers. "Leave the public houses behind. Go to your homes. Attend to your bibles this night." Beside him, James Baird nodded his agreement.

The crowd murmured unhappily, and the sheriff stepped forward again, drawing the two men into a final discussion, this time speaking too low to be heard. At the end of it, one of the redcoats was summoned forward. He took out a knife from his belt and cut the bonds that held the condemned men's wrists.

They shook off the ropes then, giving each other one last look before coming together in a tight embrace, Baird resting his forehead against Hardie's shoulder for one long moment before they parted.

"Look at them," one of the men beside David jeered. "They're like a pair o' women."

David bit his cheek till he tasted blood to stop himself from turning on the man. A woman in front of him was less controlled. She turned and hissed that they were a bunch of ignorant bastards. They told her to shut her face with the sort of good humour that could turn vicious in the blink of an eye. David didn't even look at them—he fixed his attention where it needed to be. On the scaffold.

The prisoners stood back to back, two proud, upright figures, while the hangman stepped forward to settle the nooses about their necks and black hoods over their heads. Hardie held a white handkerchief in his left hand. The hangman's signal.

For a few moments they remained thus, and the crowd seemed to hold its collective breath. Even the drunks were silent now. The condemned men groped for each other's hands, linking their fingers together in a final gesture of solidarity. The handkerchief dropped.

So did the men.

David kept his gaze on their linked hands. In that first instant it seemed to him that their fingers tightened. Gradually though, the connection loosened. Their kicking legs stilled, bodies growing limp, hands parting. Souls leaving. He knew, somehow, the precise moment at which they ceased to inhabit their bodies. And then they merely hung there, dead. Two carcasses.

A woman wailed.

"Shame!" someone else cried wildly and the cry was taken up by the crowd. *Shame! Shame! Murder!*

The cries went on and on, and the redcoats around the square began to look twitchy, their weapons quivering with readiness. The men and women that David stood among hung on the cusp of transforming into a mob—all it would take, David thought, was one rash gesture, one thrown stone, and this could be another Peterloo.

Diversion came in the form of two large men stepping forward to cut down the bodies. Gradually, the cries began to die away as the crowd strained forward, waiting for the next stage in the proceedings. The headsman.

They settled Hardie's body on the block first, and the headsman stepped forward. He looked surprisingly small, slight even. A spectator had claimed earlier that this was the same man who'd beheaded the body of James Wilson, another of the radicals, a week earlier. A medical student, the spectator had claimed, skilled in dissection.

When the headsman lifted the axe, an agonised cry from someone in the crowd fractured the silence. Perhaps it put him off. Or perhaps it was inexperience—it wasn't as though there was much call for headsmen these days, after all. Whatever the case, it took him three blows to remove Hardie's head and two for Baird's. After each operation, he held up the head, gore dripping gruesomely from the neck, and declared, "This is the head of a traitor!" And each time, the spectators howled, like a great beast bellowing, half in pain, half in protest.

A group of men moved onto the scaffold then, to lift the bodies into coffins and load them onto a wagon for removal.

There was nothing left for the crowd to witness now, other than the inevitable clearing up. Halfway through the operation, the bored spectators began to disperse. It happened more peaceably than David could've imagined possible, as though when the headsman struck with his axe, he'd struck at the incipient mob amongst them.

Even the drunken fools beside David who'd been thrumming with barely suppressed violence throughout the whole proceedings had finally subsided. They turned from the scaffold with deadened expressions, calm now, and melted away with the rest of the departing crowd.

David waited, though. He waited for the wagon to be loaded up, then watched it slowly trundle away, rattling over uneven cobbles. Still he waited. Till the wagon was completely out of sight. Until James and Andrew were gone forever.

Only then did he turn away and walk back to the inn.

CHAPTER TWO

Despite Andrew Hardie's exhortation to the crowd to go home and read their bibles, the town's public houses were full that night, their customers toasting the dead men, for the most part.

David was staying one more night at the inn before taking the coach back to Edinburgh in the morning and when he went down to the taproom, he found the place bustling with custom, not a free chair in sight.

The landlady spotted him hovering in the doorway. "Good evenin' to you, Mr. Lauriston," she said in a carrying voice, causing a large group of men in plain working clothes to look around at the new arrival. They sized him up, taking in his well-made clothes with suspicious expressions.

"Good evening, Mrs. Fairbairn," David replied, painfully aware of his refined voice. Dropping his old dialect and adopting the King's English had been a necessity for his profession, but at times like this, it made him self-conscious.

"Are you wanting some dinner?" she asked politely.

"Ah, yes, please."

"Come away into the back parlour where it's less busy, then."

She came out from behind the bar, and he followed her out of the crowded taproom and into a cold and empty back parlour dominated by an enormous mahogany dining table. It was quiet and empty of people. Much fancier than the taproom and much less snug.

"I'll have Katy come and light the fire. What are you wanting for dinner? I've got a nice meat pie."

"That sounds excellent." In truth, the thought of food left him cold, but it was better than sitting in his chamber all night.

"Ale?"

"Yes, please."

"I'll be back in a minute." She bustled away while David took a seat at the gleaming table.

The furniture in here was much better quality than in the taproom, where well-worn benches and ancient scarred tables were the order of the day. The long dining table shone as though it was polished often. Mrs. Fairbairn's pride and joy, he guessed. It was empty but for a stub of tallow candle on a pewter plate in the centre. A few other candles flickered on a sideboard. Beyond the door, David could hear the chatter of patrons from the taproom, occasional bursts of laughter, a dog barking. He felt a stab of loneliness, followed by one of foolishness. Was he a child to mind a bit of solitude?

After a few minutes, the girl, Katy, slinked in. She was only thirteen or so, a wee slip of a thing weighed down by a heavy coal scuttle. She looked terrified when David greeted her, mumbling something he couldn't make out before turning to the fireplace to kneel down and scrape out the grate before laying a fresh fire.

She was just finishing up when Mrs. Fairbairn entered again. With her was a tall, well-dressed gentleman, the quality of his coat and boots unmistakable even in this poor light.

"Come away in, sir," the landlady said as the maidservant

scuttled past them. "Make yourself comfortable. This gentleman is Mr. Lauriston, my other guest."

The man turned towards David with a polite smile. His dark gaze moved over David with candid interest, and it seemed to David that his smile grew as he took in what he saw, becoming faintly predatory. David's heartbeat quickened in response, rising to struggle like a trapped bird at the base of his throat. Discomfited, and annoyed at himself for his reaction, he nodded more curtly than he ordinarily would.

"Pleased to meet you, Mr. Lauriston," the man said. "Do you mind if I join you for dinner?" His accent was the accent of the very rich Scot. Cut-glass English with just the slightest lilt. Over six feet in height, almost a full head taller than David, and far broader.

"No, of course not, Mr.—?"

"Balfour. Murdo Balfour."

They shook hands. Balfour had removed his gloves, and the brief, icy clasp of his fingers chilled David's own. He could still feel the ghost of their grasp once Balfour had released him.

Balfour turned away to hang his coat and hat on a stand in the corner of the room while Mrs. Fairbairn readied the table. Lifting the tallow candle stub, she set it aside and fetched a white bundle from the sideboard. With a shake of her arms, the bundle opened up like the sail of a ship catching the wind and settled over the dark wood in soft folds. She finished the table with a branch of beeswax candles, lighting them with a flame borrowed from the crackling fire.

David glanced surreptitiously at Balfour as he settled himself into a chair. He was perhaps thirty or so. Not classically handsome, but arresting, with bold, startling features. His thick hair looked black but might be very dark brown—difficult to tell in this light—and his complexion was fashionably pale. It was a startling combination with all that height and a pair of shoulders on him that had surely brushed the sides of the doorway when he walked in here. Straight nose, dark brows, a wide, sardonic mouth with a twist to it that suggested the man spent his life laughing at his fellow man. Not a particularly friendly face but a compelling one. And right now, David realised—dismayed to notice Balfour had just caught him cataloguing his features—one that was animated with what appeared to be veiled amusement.

The man's dark gaze was very direct. Meeting it, David felt a surge of something that was part excitement, part alarm. *Could he be...?* David damned the question even as it arose in his mind. He wasn't looking for company tonight. He wasn't. It had been many months since his last lapse.

"What is your direction, Mr. Lauriston?" Balfour's tone was neutral, but his gaze seemed to linger a little on David's mouth. Or was David imagining things?

"I am due to return to the capital tomorrow. And you?" David kept his voice cool.

"It appears we are taking different roads. I am bound for Argyllshire."

A boy entered the dining room. He placed a jug of ale and two pewter cups on the table and hurried off again, leaving the men to help themselves.

Balfour poured ale for them both and offered his cup in a toast. "To safe journeys."

David echoed his words obligingly.

The ale was surprisingly decent. A pale ale, the colour of weak tea, hoppy and cool. They both drank deeply, and Balfour filled their cups again.

"Did you see the hanging today?" Balfour asked as he poured, eyes on the jug.

David managed to repress his urge to shudder, though only just. "Yes," he said. "Though it wasn't just a hanging."

"No, they were beheaded too, I heard. Treason, wasn't it? A pair of radicals?"

David nodded and drank again. "You were not there?" he

asked when he placed his cup back on the table.

Balfour shook his head. "I've only just arrived in town."

David took the opportunity to change the subject. "And where have you come from, Mr. Balfour?"

"London."

"A long journey," David observed. Odd, he thought, to come through Stirling on the way to Argyllshire, but he made no comment on that.

"I'm used to it. I've lived in London for a number of years now, but my family home is in Argyllshire, and I'm back at least once a year."

"I guessed you were a Scot," David admitted, "though your accent is difficult to place."

"So I'm told." Balfour gave a thin smile. "Most of my own countrymen think I'm English."

Most of them would. But David came across men like this all the time—wealthy Scots who preferred to spend their time in London, where the real political power was. He'd wager that the home in Argyllshire was a large estate. Balfour seemed like the sort of man used to having his own way, and the carelessly confident way he'd looked David over fitted with that.

The boy returned, carrying two heaped plates of meat pie and a dish of roasted vegetables. He set the dishes down before them wordlessly and hurried off to his next task. David stared down at the golden pie crust and pool of thick brown gravy and wondered why he'd ordered the meal. His already poor appetite had deserted him entirely now.

"This smells good," Balfour said conversationally. He tucked in with gusto. He probably had to eat a lot with that big, brawny body.

They made civil conversation while they ate, enquiring after one another's journeys and commenting on weather, which they agreed looked like imminent rain. The topics they chose were safe and bland, and gradually David's edginess began to ebb a little.

Once he'd forced down half of his dinner, David pushed his plate aside.

"Aren't you hungry?" Balfour asked.

"Not really." David took a long draught of ale, wishing he'd asked for some whisky as well. The ale was too light—it didn't even touch him. He felt raw and too sober. He kept seeing Baird's and Hardie's linked hands, their bodies jerking against the rope. The moment he realised they were gone.

A wave of intense sadness and loneliness swamped him. Was this all there was? A few brief moments of connection— the grasp of another's hand on the scaffold—and then you were cast out, alone, into the great universe?

Balfour's voice, rising in a question, drew him back to the world.

"I'm sorry, I didn't catch that," David admitted, mortified by the heat he felt creeping into his cheeks.

"I was asking how you occupy yourself day to day, Mr. Lauriston." Balfour looked David in the eye as he spoke, his gaze disconcertingly direct. He didn't seem to obey the normal rules of social conversation. Wasn't it terribly unusual to stare so? Or was David seeing things that weren't there?

"I am a member of the Faculty of Advocates," David said. Even now, that announcement gave him a small, prideful thrill, though something about Balfour's answering smile took away a little of David's pleasure.

"Ah, a lawyer," Balfour said with a raised brow. "A noble profession."

Why did David get the sense that Balfour meant the exact opposite of what he said? He considered pointing that out, but at the last moment decided not to and took another mouthful of ale to swallow the words down with. Balfour grinned, and for some reason, David had the unsettling feeling the man had followed his train of thought.

"I practice mainly civil law," David said after a moment, aware of the tightness in his voice, "Though I have recently been involved in some criminal cases."

"Is that so? I may look you up when I am next in Edinburgh. I have a few legal matters that I need attended to."

"I am an advocate, Mr. Balfour. I only deal with court cases. If you need a will or some property deeds drawn up, you will need to engage a solicitor, though I would be happy to recommend someone."

Balfour gave him a long, unsmiling look. "I know what an advocate is, Mr. Lauriston."

Again, David felt discomfited. "I apologise," he said stiffly, "it's just that people often confuse the two professions." Now he sounded pompous.

"No need to apologise," Balfour replied easily, returning his attention to his plate. "This is an excellent pie," he added, changing the subject. He glanced at David's half-eaten effort. "It's a crime to leave so much uneaten."

"I'm afraid I'm not especially hungry."

"With the greatest respect, you look as though you could use a bit of feeding up."

"You sound like my mother," David replied before he could think better of it.

Balfour laughed at David's waspish tone, his mouth curving, a deep dimple flashing in his cheek. "Well, mothers are usually right about these things." The laughter lines at the corners of his dark eyes crinkled when he laughed, making him look suddenly much less cynical and worldly.

That infinitesimal change in expression inexplicably lightened David's mood; he gave a reluctant laugh of his own. "She gets annoyed with me when I forget to eat," he admitted.

"You forget to *eat*?"

Balfour sounded so horrified that David couldn't help but laugh again. "Not for long, but I do miss the odd meal. I'm not married, you see. It's easily done when I'm working—I lose track of the time."

Balfour gave him another of those direct, amused looks. "Now, why am I not surprised to hear that you're a bachelor, Mr. Lauriston?"

That was an odd thing to say, David thought. What did he mean by it? David didn't want to jump to unwarranted conclusions, but he couldn't help but wonder if the man shared David's own inclinations.

Balfour leaned forward, his intent gaze fixed on David. "Tell me, Mr. Lauriston—" But before he could say more, the door opened again. This time it was Mrs. Fairbairn, come to clear the plates away. Balfour sighed and leaned back in his chair.

"I've got a suet pudding if you'd like, gentlemen?" she told them, looking disappointed when they both declined.

As she walked away, laden with dishes, David realised that this meant the meal was over and was surprised at how the thought dismayed him. Just as the landlady reached the door, he called out impulsively, "Mrs. Fairbairn—"

She looked over her shoulder, a question in her eyes.

"Could you bring us some whisky?"

She nodded. "Of course. I'll be back directly."

Only after the door closed behind her did it occur to David that he ought to have asked Balfour first if he wanted to join him. He glanced at the other man. "I'm sorry, that was presumptuous of me. Please don't feel obliged to join me if you'd rather go to bed."

"Not at all," the other man said. "I quite fancy a whisky myself. I only drink the stuff when I'm in Scotland, and the first dram is always the best."

Moments later, the landlady was back with two small jugs, one of whisky and one of water, and two dram glasses. She poured the two men a generous nip each and left the rest on the table, promising, at David's insistence, to add the cost to David's bill. As soon as she was gone, David threw back the first measure, relishing the burn down his gullet. Balfour was right, the first dram was always the best.

He poured himself another, fighting the urge to throw that back too, letting it sit in the glass untouched. He told himself he'd not take another drink till Balfour had finished his own dram, but that was easier said than done. Balfour sipped slowly, contemplatively, his long body relaxed and comfortable.

At last David gave in. He picked up the second measure and swallowed that too, setting his glass down with a small bang on the mahogany table. He made no immediate move to replenish his glass, but his forbearance was to no avail—Balfour picked up the jug this time and topped David's small glass off, doubling the measure this time.

"Before the landlady came in, I was about to ask you something," Balfour said as he added a little water to his own glass, diluting the spirit.

"Oh yes? What was that?"

Balfour smiled, as relaxed as though he were proposing a game of cards. His dark gaze grew languid and inviting. "Do you really need to ask?"

David's heart began to race. He was almost sure what Balfour was alluding to, but there remained a hint of doubt, and the dangers attendant upon such misunderstandings were great.

"I would appreciate some—clarification," David replied carefully.

Balfour's grin deepened. "How's this, then? I noticed the way you've been looking at me."

David flushed at this directness but forced himself to keep looking at Balfour, despite his burning cheeks.

Balfour leaned back in his seat, appearing supremely comfortable. "And I know that look very well. I believe I know what manner of man you are, Mr. Lauriston."

David bristled a little both at the man's easy assumption and at how he expressed it. Had David really been staring at him all that much? He was usually so careful. Perhaps his defences were lower than usual today. Or perhaps it was Murdo Balfour—the man made David feel supremely off-balance.

"You don't know anything about me," David said, determined to restore a polite distance. "We've only just met."

He expected Balfour to back off then, put off by David's refusal to bite. But he didn't. Quite the opposite. Instead he put his elbows on the mahogany table and leaned forward, his dark gaze fixed on David.

"I may not know you," Balfour said softly. "But I'm confident that you and I are similar, in certain ways."

"I don't know what—"

"Come now," Balfour interrupted, more gently this time. "We are fellow travellers, heading in opposite directions. Just passing ships. Tomorrow we will be gone and will not meet again. There is nothing to fear from letting your guard down a little."

David stared at him helplessly. "You don't know me," he repeated, though less firmly this time.

"I think I do, a little. The part that's similar to me anyway."

David didn't respond to that, but perhaps the fear he felt at being so easily discovered showed on his face—for the first time, Balfour's expression grew troubled.

"I'm sorry if I've offended you," he said. "I mean no insult. Quite the opposite. The truth is..."He paused, as though considering precisely what that truth might be. "I can't remember the last time someone intrigued me as you do."

He spoke the words as easily as you like, quite conversational as he leaned back in his chair and his dark eyes wandered over David's tense form. Then he smiled, a wide attractive smile. "And it has to be said—you're the prettiest lad I've seen in a long time."

"*Pretty?*" David protested, mortified, but even as he rejected Balfour's assessment, it reached some part of him, buried deep, that was like parched earth. He searched Balfour's face for contempt or shame. Mockery. But there was none, and nothing furtive either. Nothing furtive or careful or even goddamned *prudent*. What was Balfour thinking to speak to a man, a stranger, as he was speaking to David? It was so reckless that David would have suspected some kind of trap if their meeting could have been anything other than sheer coincidence.

David stared at the other man, breath held as he considered his reply. There was something raw and powerful in Balfour's dark gaze. David saw desire and determination. He saw that Balfour wanted him.

Beyond anything else, that decided him.

He was going to lapse again.

He would hate himself in the morning, but that didn't matter right now. After several tense heartbeats, he dropped his gaze and muttered, "We can't do it here. The walls between the chambers are paper thin."

"Come with me," Balfour replied. "I know a place."

Outside the inn, there was a faint mizzle of freezing rain. David huddled deeper into his coat. It was a dark and moonless night, every star in the sky obscured by clouds.

"This way," Balfour whispered. He tugged at David's sleeve, drawing him towards a nearby alley. David considered resisting for an instant, alarmed by Balfour's straightforwardness, his apparent disregard for risk. But in the end, David allowed himself to be led, half manhandled, actually, into a narrow close so dark he could no longer see the other man's face.

Balfour pulled David deep into the close before he stopped and turned towards him. He backed him into the cold, damp wall, and David let himself be pushed, welcoming Balfour's bulk and certainty.

The close smelled of piss and rotting refuse, but when Balfour crowded into David, he banished those smells. He smelled clean and healthy and male, and David inhaled deeply as his cheek pressed against David's own, experiencing a moment of intense excitement at the combination of sensations—Balfour's scent, the power and warmth of his body, the faint roughness of his jaw. Even so, when Balfour's lips sought his own, David turned his head away, reaching instead for the placket of the other man's breeches.

Balfour gave a soft laugh. "You object to kissing?" he murmured in David's ear. The heat of his breath sent a shiver down David's flank. "Such a shame. Your mouth was made to be kissed."

David made an impatient noise of rejection at that absurd declaration. The compliment was almost enough to put him off his stride altogether. But having agreed to come out here, casting all his reservations aside, he was determined to make it worth it and refused to be distracted. His busy fingers undid the buttons of Balfour's breeches, and his hands slid inside, pushing down the other man's drawers to expose his swelling cock. When David grasped the thick shaft, Balfour gave a deep sigh of pleasure that gusted against the side of David's face.

David lightly caressed the hard rod of flesh, then let his

fingers drift down to the balls hanging below. The man's cock was like velvet, the prickle of hair on his scrotum a provoking contrast that made David's pulse pound and breath come quick. David closed his fingers around Balfour's prick again and dragged upwards. A bead of moisture on the tip spread stickily under David's thumb while Balfour murmured incoherent encouragement.

The wall was cold at David's back, but Balfour radiated heat and strength. For a few brief moments, David allowed himself to enjoy without guilt the feeling of being warmed and protected, but that was not a weakness he would allow himself to indulge in for long. Instead he dropped to his knees, enveloping the plump head of Balfour's cock in his mouth and quickly swallowing the length down.

The cobbles under his knees were hard and wet, but he didn't care. He took Balfour to the back of his throat, loving the way the man filled his mouth, the pulse of musky flesh pressing insistently on his soft palate. Above him, Balfour groaned and his long, strong fingers tunnelled into David's hair, dragging on the short silky strands. David's hat was gone, probably sitting in a puddle. He didn't give a damn. All he cared about was this. Bringing Balfour to completion in his mouth. Even if David didn't climax now, he would be able to do so later, just from remembering this.

His own cock was painful in his breeches, swollen with desire but constricted by the tight fabric and his kneeling position. In an odd way, he relished the uncomfortable sensation. Strangely it almost enhanced the delight of pleasing Balfour. And he was pleasing him, if the man's moans were anything to go by. Balfour's fingers tightened on David's skull as he began to reach his crisis, his cock thickening and hardening just a fraction more. David consciously stilled and opened his jaw and throat as well as he could.

"Christ," Balfour moaned. "Yes, that's good."

And then Balfour was fucking his mouth in short, efficient

jabs. David did his best to stay still, to accommodate all that hammering flesh. He tried to spare Balfour the scrape of his teeth but it was impossible to avoid the occasional catch and the resultant loss of rhythm. Impossible too not to gag, not to choke and drool a little. But it didn't matter. Somehow, it was the imperfections of this that made it so very good.

Balfour stiffened and froze, his cock right at the back of David's throat now. And all David needed to endure was one long, last breathless moment as the other man jerked out his crisis, spilling his semen down David's willing throat. David's head swam, vision blurring. He felt an odd sort of ecstasy in his physical discomfort, a muddling up of his honest worship of Balfour's body with a deep-rooted belief that he deserved nothing more. Pleasure and torment together.

When Balfour finally withdrew his prick, David stayed where he was, half expecting the other man to do up his breeches and walk away. It wouldn't be the first time. But before David knew where he was, Balfour had yanked him to his feet and pressed him back against the wall. And then Balfour's lips were on his, his tongue pressing inside, tasting hungrily.

Still dazed, and now weak with longing, he didn't turn away this time, but allowed Balfour to ravish his mouth.

After a while, the bigger man drew back a little, his mouth gentling. David almost regretted allowing the kiss because he knew one day soon he would look back at this moment and wish he'd been strong enough to turn away from it. But for now he pushed that thought to the back of his mind and returned Balfour's kiss, revelling in the conflicting sensations of warm, soft lips and rough, scraping jaw.

Eventually, Balfour broke the kiss and pulled away, smiling, a glint of teeth that David could just make out in the darkness.

"I think that was the best cock-sucking I've ever had," he

said. The crudity of his words was softened by their teasing tone and that shadowy, piratical smile. His hands moved lower, tracing the shape of David's backside. "I only wish I could fuck you."

David shivered, saying nothing. That, he would never allow. Thankfully it seemed the danger of it was past now. He distracted himself from the uncomfortable thought by throwing his head back against the wet bricks while Balfour unbuttoned his breeches and drew out his aching member.

Stroking David's prick with one hand, Balfour yanked at his cravat with the other, exposing David's throat, his mouth descending in a hot kiss that turned into a bite and then a kiss again.

"Yes, yes, God please—" David muttered, hips jerking as pleasure and need built intolerably. A powerful climax brewed at the base of his spine as Balfour's mouth savaged his throat again and his big hand worked. His brawny body shoved at David, warm and assertive, pushing him harder into the wall. Demanding and taking. David was being conquered by a relentless force. Routed utterly.

Balfour kissed up the line of David's throat and whispered harshly in his ear, "God, but I want to do everything to you. I want you in my hand. I want you in my mouth. I want to bury my tongue inside you and fuck you forever."

Christ.

David's orgasm, when it came, was the most intense he could remember. And through it all, Balfour was there, enveloping David with his warmth and strength.

For a few moments after, they stood, David's head resting on the other man's shoulder as he came back to himself. The blissful aftershocks gradually faded away and he became aware, once again, of the cold wall behind him, the dreich, mizzling rain.

Balfour brought out a handkerchief and used it to clean David up, his smile glinting again in the darkness. David felt embarrassed by the attention, but when Balfour tucked the handkerchief away and began to attend to his own breeches, he experienced the oddest sense of loss. After they'd fastened themselves up and David had roughly retied his cravat, Balfour bent down, straightening again with David's hat in his hand.

"I wouldn't put it on if I were you," he said, offering it to David.

"No," David agreed with a weak smile, taking it. God only knew what was on the ground under their feet.

They exited the close together and paused at the opening onto the street.

"I'll let you go ahead," Balfour said.

David nodded briskly, hiding the melancholy that had suddenly settled on him like an old familiar coat. "Good night then," he said. He began to turn away.

"Lauriston—"

He stilled at the sound of his name on the other man's lips and looked over his shoulder. All he could see in the darkness was Balfour's bulky outline, yet even without seeing his expression, David somehow sensed a hesitance in him.

"Yes?"

"That was—good. I hope it was for you too?"

David swallowed, wondering why that simple question should make his chest ache so.

Before he could answer, the door of the inn burst open and a group of men exploded onto the street, talking and laughing loudly. The light and noise broke the strange fragile spell between them.

David imagined going to Balfour, pressing his lips against the other man's and whispering in his ear, *Yes, it was good. Better than good.* And, *Come to bed with me. Stay the night.*

Instead he nodded once, his expression carefully blank. "Good night, Mr. Balfour."

Once inside, he went straight up to his chamber where he

stripped off his clothes and got into bed. There he lay, awake, reliving every second of that brief, intense, unexpected encounter, before finally falling into a fitful sleep in the early hours. By the time he woke the next morning, Murdo Balfour was long gone.

CHAPTER THREE

"David Lauriston! Where on earth have you been this last week?"

David looked up from his books, blinking. Francis Jeffrey was sliding into the seat on the other side of the desk. Short, dark-haired, bright-eyed and smiling. A small package, Mr. Jeffrey, but a big man in other ways.

"Mr. Jeffrey, how are you?" David spoke more softly. The library was quiet this morning, but a handful of other advocates were working studiously at their desks.

"Don't avoid the question, dear fellow," Jeffrey replied, one dark eyebrow raised. "Where have you been?"

David busied himself marking his page with a slip of paper and closing his book. "I went away for a few days," he said mildly. "Has anything interesting happened in my absence?"

Jeffrey cocked his head to the side like a spry little bird and stared at David for several long moments. David felt his cheeks heat but stayed carefully mute. Eventually, the other man sighed dramatically. "I can guess anyway. You went to see the execution, didn't you?"

David said nothing, but he knew his complexion betrayed

him. Inwardly he cursed his fair skin and red hair—his colouring gave rise to the worst sort of painfully red blushes.

"In a way, I admire you, Lauriston," Jeffrey said. "But don't imagine this hasn't been noted."

"I didn't see anyone there—"

"I don't mean the execution—though thank you for confirming my suspicions—I mean your attachment to the case." He gave one of his twitchy little smiles. "Don't misunderstand me. I valued your contribution very highly, and believe me, I'm mindful of how modest a fee you took. But I don't want to see your progress at the Bar suffer more than it needs to, and the fact is, my boy, you have allowed your sympathy for our clients to show too plainly. It is imprudent to espouse such views in our profession."

"I never espoused any views," David protested.

"You were openly sympathetic. It is enough."

"And so were you."

"Ah, but I am Francis Jeffrey." He preened a little as he said it, but it was true. He was Francis Jeffrey, the famous man of letters, still overlooked from time to time because of his Whig leanings, but with a fearsome reputation that made sure he had no shortage of cases. Not these days, anyway.

Working with him on the weavers' case had been a privilege, even though David's fee had indeed been modest. He'd offered his services as junior counsel on something of a whim, keen for the opportunity to work with the great man. He hadn't considered how consuming the case was going to be. Now he urgently needed to pick up some new cases and earn some fees, if he was to pay his rent on time.

David smiled. "Thank you for your concern. But I'm fine."

"Are you?" the older man asked, one sceptical brow raised. "I know what it's like to be where you are now. Trying to make a reputation when it feels like no one will give you a chance. I've had thin years—good lord, thin *decades*—thanks to my political sympathies."

"Well, you seem to have done all right for yourself," David replied lightly. "If that house of yours in the country is any measure."

Jeffrey gave his high, chirping laugh—he loved to be teased about his new house. "Craigcrook was obtained with the fruits of my writing, dear boy. And stop changing the subject. My point is this: I had years of scraping around for work, and it's not what I'd wish for you. You're a very able fellow. I'd like to see you get on."

David sighed. "Getting new cases isn't easy, but I'm not destitute yet."

Jeffrey sniffed. "You need to play the game, boy. Get to know more of the senior chaps. If they like you, they'll bring you into their cases and they'll introduce you to the solicitors who instruct them."

"That's easier said than done."

"I know," Jeffrey replied. "And my reputation isn't much help to you, I'm afraid, but some of my friends could be of more assistance to you. So here's the thing—I mean to introduce you to some of them."

David blinked, taken aback. "That's very kind of you," he said after a pause. "Thank you."

Jeffrey looked pleased. "Excellent. So are you able to dine with us on Saturday evening? At Craigcrook?"

David paused. The idea of attending a formal dinner was unappealing, but Jeffrey was right; he had to make an effort. He forced himself to smile and answered, "I am, thank you. I'll look forward to it."

"Let's say six o'clock, then. We're a long way out of town, so we'd be pleased if you'd stay the night too."

"Th-thank you." David flushed, a little embarrassed by that suggestion, undoubtedly prompted by the awkwardness of David having neither a horse nor carriage to his name.

Jeffrey dismissed David's gratitude with a wave of his hand. "So what's this you're working on?" he asked, peering down at David's notes on the desk, at the hand-drawn map David had made in an attempt to understand the long-running boundary dispute he'd been working on.

David began to explain the facts of the case. The case had come from Stewart & Stewart, a solicitors' firm he'd clerked for while he studied. Their clients were not wealthy, but the kindly young Mr. Stewart—who at seven and fifty remained very much the junior partner to his ancient father—had provided a steady stream of small instructions to David over the last several years. In gratitude, David provided his services more cheaply than he could strictly afford. He'd already ploughed five times the hours into this problem than he'd ever dream of charging.

Jeffrey was scowling over David's map when a clerk approached the desk.

"Mr. Lauriston, I'm sorry to interrupt, sir—"

David looked up. "No need to apologise, Thomas. What is it?"

"There's a lad asking for you, sir. He wouldn't give a name. He's waiting in the hall."

David frowned. "He wouldn't give you a name? What does he look like?"

"A young fellow. Eighteen or so, I'd say. Respectable looking."

David's chair scraped the floor as he stood. "Would you excuse me, Jeffrey? I think it might be the clerk from Stewart & Stewart." Even as he uttered these words, they sounded implausible to him. Why would the solicitors' clerk not give Thomas his name?

Jeffrey waved him off, still holding the map, now comparing it with David's handwritten notes, his dark eyebrows creased in concentration.

David left him to it, following Thomas out of the library and into the great Parliament Hall, which was dim today, illuminated only by a few flickering candles in the wall sconces.

Even in this poor light, though, it was awe inspiring, the grey stone walls soaring up to a high, vaulted ceiling. Two advocates paced up and down, their footsteps echoing in counterpoint with their hushed conversation. The only other occupant was a man in the far corner. He sat, still and silent, his face obscured by the brim of his hat.

Thomas pointed at the seated figure. "That's him."

David thanked him and began walking towards his visitor, his boot heels clicking on the wooden floor. He tried to puzzle out the man's identity as he drew closer, but it was only when he stood and removed his hat that, finally, David realised who it was.

"Euan MacLennan," he said, stretching out his hand, not bothering to hide his surprise. "What brings you here?"

The young man who stood before him gave an uncertain smile, taking the hand that David offered in a brief tentative grip, his gloveless hand icy cold. He was in his early twenties, but he looked as young as the library clerk had suggested with his very fair hair and his earnest, beardless face. His ill-fitting coat added to the overall impression of awkward youthfulness; it was all wrong on his lanky frame—a mite too short in the sleeves and a mite too broad in the shoulders.

"Hello, Davy."

Davy. The use of David's given name—in its most intimate form—took him momentarily aback. But of course, it was he who had insisted Euan use it. A gesture of solidarity to the weavers and their families. Jeffrey hadn't commented at the time, but David knew he hadn't approved. He was always *Mr. Jeffrey* to them.

"I hope you don't mind me calling on you here?" Euan continued, a little breathlessly. "I didn't know how else to find you." His diction was as careful as David's own had been a few years ago, a slight hesitance in his speech that gave away the fact that his accent was not the one he'd been born with.

"Of course I don't mind," David replied. "I'm just surprised to see you, that's all." He paused. "How is Peter?"

The briefest flicker of emotion crossed Euan's face. He took a deep breath. "As well as can be expected. At least his sentence has been commuted. He is not to be executed now, but—"

But, Peter MacLennan was being transported. And how many convicts even survived the journey to the Antipodes?

"When does his ship depart?" David asked carefully.

Euan stared down at his hands. "Within the month."

David laid a hand on the lad's forearm. "He's a strong man. And as brave as a lion. He'll be all right, I'm sure of it."

"Aye," Euan whispered, but grief was etched in every line of his face. Peter wasn't only Euan's brother. A full decade older, he'd been surrogate father to his younger sibling. And as a time-served weaver with no wife or children of his own, he'd been able to support his brother with his studies at university.

Poor Peter. He'd been so proud of his younger brother, the university student. David remembered talking with him, late one evening before the trial.

"My brother reads Latin and Greek, Davy. Did you know that? He's going to be a minister in the Kirk one day..."

David swallowed past a sudden lump in his throat. "I'm so sorry, Euan," he said. "I know how distressing this is for you."

Euan shook his head and gave a determined sort of sniff. "Look at me, snivelling like a woman. You must think me an idiot."

"Not at all."

Euan's cheeks coloured. "Nevertheless, you must be wondering why I've come to see you."

"Let's sit down, and you can tell me."

They retreated to the bench Euan had been occupying when David had first come into the hall. Euan sat heavily and rested his elbows on his knees, his hat dangling from his fingertips, his gaze fixed forward, not looking at David, who settled beside him and waited for him to speak.

"I've been looking for the Englishman," Euan said at last.

"The Englishman?"

"Robert Lees."

David sat back, surprised. Lees had been a shadowy figure in the trial of James Baird and Andrew Hardie. The mysterious Englishman was believed by the weavers, whose ranks he'd joined, to be one of a number of government agents sent to Scotland with orders to stir up the brief summer uprising and flush out troublemakers. The efforts of Lees and his fellow agents had resulted in dozens of men being transported, and three—Hardie and Baird included—being executed.

And now Euan MacLennan was looking for the man? A trained agent who had already shown himself capable of the worst sort of deceit?

A lamb may as well go looking for a wolf.

"That does not sound wise," David said. "Why are you looking for him?"

Euan frowned at the wooden floor for several long moments. "I want to confront him," he said at last. "He's the reason Peter's rotting in gaol, the reason he's going to be thrown onto a transport ship in chains. The least he can do is look me in the eye and, and—" He broke off, a muscle jerking in his cheek.

"And what?"

Euan turned his head and looked at David, grief stricken. "Tell me why he did it."

Why.

It was an entirely pointless question, and yet David understood how it would torment the lad. He thought of himself all those years ago, writing letter after letter to Will Lennox asking why he'd broken off their friendship so irrevocably. Will had never answered a single one of those letters.

It took time for the burning desire for an answer to fade away, but fade it did, once you accepted you'd never know.

"Davy, please, I need your help," Euan was saying now, his tone driven. "I know you care—more than any of the others. When you first came to speak to us, I saw you were different. Like us. You learned our names, and you gave us your own. And when they handed down the verdicts, I saw your face, Davy. You felt as sick as I did."

"Of course I care," David replied sincerely. "But I don't understand what you think I can do for you."

"I've got a lead on Lees. I think he might be here in Edinburgh, circulating in your world."

"My world?" David shook his head. "If you imagine I can introduce you to someone who has dealings with government agents, you are very much mistaken. I have entry only to the very outermost circles of the legal world—not to the corridors of political power."

"I know that," Euan said. "Just hear me out, all right?"

"All right," David sighed. "Go on."

Euan took a deep breath and began again. "There was an occasion, weeks before the uprising, when Lees got drunk with Peter and told him about a woman—a woman he said he loved. Isabella is her name. She lives here in Edinburgh, and Lees told Peter her father is an advocate by profession—an advocate, like you, Davy! Lees said he was going to go and see her father in person to persuade him to let Lees marry the girl."

David watched the younger man, observing his excitement and how he tried to hide it behind a calm, measured mask.

"So you see, Lees might be in Edinburgh right now. And even if he is not, if you help me find out who this Isabella is, I might be able to find out where he has gone. There cannot be

34

too many advocates with daughters called Isabella, can there?" He finished his speech all in a rush, gabbling it out on a single breath, his voice closing up as he reached the end of his question.

The lad's desperation was awful. This was not a lead, David thought. It was a fantasy. A delusion. It didn't seem conceivable that a government agent would spill out secrets about his romantic passions to one of the men he was deceiving. And even if he had let something slip, he surely wouldn't be stupid enough to go and act on it later?

"You should forget this," David said quietly, "and go back to your studies. That is what your brother would want."

"I can't. I have to do this."

"It won't help Peter."

"I know," Euan said. "Nevertheless, I have to."

"You won't find this man, and your studies will falter—and what would Peter think of that? He would be devastated."

Euan took a deep breath, visibly calming himself. "I'm only asking you for a little help, Davy. A name, an address. That's all."

"It's not all. I would have to make enquiries, and my sympathies have already been remarked upon—"

"Please Davy. Help me." The young man's voice was husky, all pride abandoned now.

David sighed. It really was completely pointless, but he'd never been able to walk away from a plea for help. *"You're soft, laddie."* That was what his father used to say.

Besides, there was only one cure for what ailed Euan MacLennan: failure. There was nothing like failure for eroding hope, nothing else in the world. Waiting for months —years—for a letter that would never, ever come.

"All right," he sighed. "I will try to find out who this Isabella is—"

"Thank you! I knew I could—"

"But—" David held a hand up to stay Euan's babbling gratitude. "In return, you will agree to give up on this scheme if my enquiries bear no fruit."

"Yes, anything."

"And, if we do learn anything, you will do nothing —*nothing*—without first telling me, because make no mistake, Euan, this Lees is a very dangerous man."

"Yes," Euan agreed hurriedly. "Of course, anything you say, Davy." His smile was like sunshine breaking through clouds. Hope and optimism and belief blazed in his blue eyes.

All David felt was an uneasy worry in his gut.

CHAPTER FOUR

On Saturday, David walked out to Jeffrey's home at Craigcrook. It was a few miles northwest of the city, and he did it at a brisk pace, relishing the exercise and the gradual improvement of the air from the dark murk of the Old Town where he lived and worked, to the elegant but still reeky New Town, and farther out on the road to Queensferry.

He liked best the point at which the city seemed to lose its grip on the land, the buildings diminishing in size and gradually petering out until they were no longer part of the city at all but little hamlets of their own. Best of all was the last stretch, after he turned off the main road and took the road to Craigcrook.

It was dusk by this time, and it felt like he was in the country proper. Birds twittered from tree to tree, searching for a roost for the night, and the uneven dirt-packed road beneath his feet felt like home. It felt good to walk on the earth instead of on cobbles, good to experience silence and solitude. For the first seventeen years of his life, he'd lived on his father's farm, working long days at the old man's side with his brother Drew. He missed those days sometimes— being outdoors, being connected to the land and the seasons

—and now he slowed his pace to a stroll the better to enjoy the old, familiar feeling.

As he walked, David mentally ticked off the names of the members of the faculty he'd already positively excluded as having any possible connection to "Isabella". More than half already, and he'd only been making his enquiries for a few days. So far it was all exactly as he'd expected but that didn't make it a pointless exercise. Euan wanted—needed—to do something for his brother. David understood that, and he would do what he could to help, even if all it amounted to was snipping off the last thread of hope the lad had.

Besides, it would help take his mind off the other thing that had been playing on his mind all week—his encounter with Murdo Balfour. Whenever he ceased actively thinking of something else, his mind would sneak back to that memory, lingering on the recollected pleasure of their encounter in the dark close till he realised what he was doing and determinedly banished it once again.

David was accustomed to reliving his rare encounters with other men. Usually, though, he was mired in regret as he did so. This memory was different. Much as he tried to concentrate on what it had felt like to kneel on the filthy wet ground and give in to his abiding weakness, what he kept remembering was the moment Balfour dragged him to his feet and kissed him. Balfour's warm, firm lips. His sleek tongue. His solid presence.

And not feeling alone.

David pressed his lips together and reminded himself that what he had done was a sin. There was nothing in the world that could change that. He made himself think of his parents, how disgusted they'd be at the thought of him with another man. Christ, he'd seen his father's reaction once before, hadn't he? It had only been a kiss, but just the look of horror on the old man's face had destroyed David that day.

He was so immersed in his thoughts that he almost

walked past the gate that led to Jeffrey's house. Set back from the path, it was easy to miss, a dark bit of ironwork shadowed by foliage. David gave it a shove, half expecting it to be locked, but no, it swung slowly open, the well-oiled hinges making no sound. Closing the gate behind him, he walked straight into a copse of trees, coming out the other side to emerge onto a broader path that led up to the house itself.

The house was bigger than even David had expected. A big baronial pile, its high walls were obscured by a thick layer of dark green ivy. A multitude of towers, turrets and crow-stepped gables drew the eye upwards to a sky that had already darkened to violet. A few bats flitted overhead, chittering.

Coming to a halt at the front door, David paused, wondering how Jeffrey and his wife could possibly want such a large house, just for the two of them. This was worlds away from David's life. His own rooms in the heart of the Old Town were pleasant. He had a bedchamber of his own as well as another room where he could dine and work in the evening. He even had a maidservant who came every other day to clean and lay the fires and take his laundry away. She cooked his breakfast in the little kitchen on the days she came —dinner too, some days, though he generally preferred to eat in a chop house or inn in the evening. All in all, he lived very well compared to most people.

Comfortable as it was, David's home was nothing to this great house. Hard to believe that at the same age as David, Jeffrey had been in a similar position, struggling to bring in the steady stream of work a man needed to assure his success. Perhaps that was why he'd taken on this imposing house? As a measure of success, it was undeniable. Jeffrey cocking a snook at all the Tory bigwigs who'd made his early career so difficult.

Standing on Jeffrey's stoop, David felt suddenly nervous. He was comfortable with Jeffrey himself but had only met his wife once, briefly, and he had no idea who the other guests were. He brushed his hands over his coat and straightened his hat, taking a deep breath. It's just a dinner, he told himself. Raising his fist, he firmly rapped on the door.

The female servant who answered took his hat, coat and bag, then led him into the drawing room. Jeffrey and his wife sat talking with a middle-aged couple and a young woman who looked to be their daughter.

Jeffrey spotted David hovering in the doorway and rose from his chair, his expressive face lit with a bright smile.

"Mr. Lauriston!" he exclaimed as he walked forward to greet David. "So glad you could come!" He shook David's hand and added, *sotto voce*, "I invited someone who could be useful for you to know."

He ushered David over to the rest of the group. Mrs. Jeffrey stood to greet him. It seemed she remembered him.

"Mr. Lauriston, how nice to see you again." She was a plain, sallow-skinned woman with mouse-brown hair, unassuming in her manner and easy to overlook. When she spoke, though, her distinctive American accent was warm and confident.

David took her proffered hand and bowed over it awkwardly, fretting inwardly over his pose and the correctness of the distance between her gloved hand and his face. He was always embarrassed by social niceties. He'd been taught at his father's knee to look past all that; taught that the substance of a man's character mattered more than the polish of his manners. His father—an elder of the church and a good Presbyterian—would think it absurd to judge a man by the way he held his cutlery, and for some reason, it made David feel disloyal to him whenever he tried to master such inconsequentialities.

"Allow me to introduce you to Mr. and Mrs. Chalmers and their daughter, Elizabeth," Mrs. Jeffrey said, curling her arm around David's and drawing him over to the other guests. "Though of course, you must know Mr. Chalmers already."

David realised he did recognise the paunchy, balding man who had risen from his chair as Mrs. Jeffrey approached with David in tow. Patrick Chalmers was a senior advocate, a man David had never spoken to or, he was sure, been noticed by. Highly regarded by the judges, Chalmers had no shortage of work and was an influential man in the faculty. David was surprised Jeffrey knew the man well enough to ask him to dine. They ordinarily moved in very different circles.

"Ah yes," Chalmers said, shaking the hand David offered. "Mr. Lauriston, of course." It was polite of him to pretend he knew who David was, and David was properly grateful.

"It's good to see you, sir," he replied earnestly.

"My wife, Mrs. Chalmers," the older man said, gesturing at the lady seated behind him.

David executed another inelegant bow, and Mrs. Chalmers gave a chilly sort of nod. She was a spare, grey-haired lady of around fifty years with a querulous expression that looked to be permanent. David felt rather like a leg of lamb as she looked him over assessingly.

"And my daughter, Elizabeth." Chalmers's voice warmed, his jowly face indulgent as he looked on his child, an ordinary-looking girl with dark eyes and middling-brown hair dressed in a fussy pink gown. Unlike her mother, she stood to be introduced and bobbed a little curtsey in response to his bow, giving him a shy smile.

As soon as David took a seat, Mrs. Chalmers began to question him, rude, pointed questions about his family and background, designed to ascertain his prospects, no doubt.

"Are you one of the Lauristons of St. Andrews? I know several of that family."

"No, ma'am. I'm from a small village around twenty miles from here called Midlauder."

"I've never heard of it," she said, frowning. "What do your people do there?"

David explained that his father was a tenant farmer, that the tenancy would go to David's brother eventually. As he spoke, he could tell by Mrs. Chalmers's hard stare and thin lips that she was not impressed by what she heard.

Elizabeth Chalmers was much more pleasant than her mother. Her not-quite-pretty face reminded him of his older cousin, Connie, and when they sat down to dine, she did not stay silent as so many young ladies would have done but displayed a lively interest in the wide-ranging conversation that played out over the course of the meal. By contrast, Mrs. Chalmers opined several times, when asked a direct question, that she was sure she couldn't offer a sensible opinion and that she was happy to defer to her husband—though she struck David as a lady who knew her own mind very well.

Whenever Elizabeth spoke, Mrs. Chalmers's mouth tightened with displeasure. She was the sort of woman who could make her unhappiness felt without speaking a word. The crease of her brow was eloquent, the pinch of her lips graphic. The younger woman was not cowed, though. She continued to converse with the group as a whole, ignoring her mother's antics, though her eyes flicked often towards her unhappy parent.

As for Mr. Chalmers, he seemed oblivious to his wife and beamed whenever his daughter spoke, his pride in her very evident. His approval seemed to keep Mrs. Chalmers silent, until Jeffrey raised the topic of a recent election. From there, the conversation inevitably veered onto radicals and the events earlier in the year.

"You defended those weavers, did you not, Mr. Jeffrey?" Elizabeth asked. "The ones who were executed for their part in the uprising?"

Jeffrey opened his mouth to answer but was interrupted by Mrs. Chalmers.

"When we go to London, Elizabeth—if we *ever* do—you are going to have to learn to curb your tongue at social occasions," she said sharply. "That is not an appropriate subject for polite conversation, and certainly not from a young lady!"

The conversation ground to an embarrassed halt. Elizabeth's cheeks blazed. Mr. Chalmers said nothing, though he frowned slightly at his wife. She pressed her lips together, but her expression was unapologetic. Jeffrey shifted in his chair, unsure how to react.

It was Mrs. Jeffrey who finally took control. "Come now," she said to the older lady, coaxing. "We're not in London now, thank heavens! And we've all been enjoying Miss Elizabeth's conversation immensely, isn't that right, Mr. Lauriston?"

Drawn unwillingly into acting the part of the girl's knight errant, David stammered out his agreement. "Ah—yes. The company of an intelligent woman is infinitely more enjoyable than that of a lady who has nothing to talk about other than—than—fashions and entertainments. And I do, of course, have a special interest in the case Miss Chalmers speaks of myself."

"Mr. Lauriston juniored to me on the weavers' case, Miss Chalmers," Jeffrey added smoothly, then, looking at Mr. Chalmers, added, "Excellent junior. He has a fine legal brain, and he works like a Trojan."

Mr. Chalmers glanced at David.

"You are too forbearing, Mr. Lauriston," Mrs. Chalmers complained, unwilling to give up the point. "Most gentlemen would not be so understanding."

Elizabeth stared down at her plate, saying nothing.

For the rest of the meal, she offered no other views. Even when Mrs. Jeffrey tried to draw her out with innocuous questions, her responses were quiet and brief.

When dinner was over, the ladies rose, quitting the dining room to take tea in the drawing room while the gentlemen had their port. The table seemed much larger without them, an empty chair beside each of the three men. Chalmers stretched out, looking relaxed and easy for the first time all evening.

Jeffrey poured the port the maidservant brought them. It was strong stuff, dark purplish-brown and heady with flavour. David had never drunk port much before. He was a whisky man, and he found the flavour of the fortified wine very sweet to his palate. Chalmers seemed to like it, though.

"So, Jeffrey, Mr. Lauriston here is one of your bright sparks, is he?" Chalmers asked jovially.

Jeffrey chuckled. "He is indeed. One of my protégés, though he'd do better with another sponsor, I fear."

"Oh, you do well enough," Chalmers returned drily.

"I suppose," Jeffrey replied. "Though it's taken long enough. And I've made more pennies from writing than from the law, as you know."

"From the *Edinburgh Review*? That rag!" Chalmers laughed, and Jeffrey joined him, the two of them seeming very tickled.

"Do you read Jeffrey's rag, Mr. Lauriston?" Chalmers asked when their laughter had subsided.

"Of course," David said, then added, "though Mr. Jeffrey's literary tastes do not coincide with my own."

"You presume to disagree with the great literary critic?" Chalmers asked merrily. "In what particular?"

"He thinks I was hard on Mr. Keats," Jeffrey interjected.

"With the greatest respect, you were," David said. "Mr. Keats is a genius."

"And I said so! *A beautiful imagination*, my very words!"

"*Absurd, obscure, rash.* Your very words."

Chalmers laughed. "I'm pleased to see you're not one for toadying, Mr. Lauriston. I detest a toady."

"A most important consideration, I find," Jeffrey added smoothly, "when choosing a junior advocate to work with."

Chalmers chuckled again and glanced at David. "Jeffrey

knows I'm always looking for bright juniors. I'm of a lazy disposition, you see."

"Lazy you may be, but you're the finest advocate I know," Jeffrey replied.

"All right, no need to lay it on so thick. I'll give your protégé a try." Chalmers threw back the last of his port, then fixed a surprisingly sober look on David. "And if you live up to Jeffrey's recommendation, there'll be more work, so make sure you impress me."

"Thank you, sir," David said, blinking in surprise. "I'm grateful for the opportunity."

"No need to thank me now," Chalmers replied. "If you do well, you can take one of my daughters off my hands. I've got three more besides Elizabeth."

David flushed, and the other two men laughed.

Soon after, they rose and joined the ladies.

It seemed Jeffrey was not the only host with a purpose. Mrs. Jeffrey appeared to be cherishing some matchmaking ambitions. When the gentlemen entered the drawing room, she ushered David and Elizabeth Chalmers over to the pianoforte and suggested they select some music for Elizabeth to play. The two older couples she herded to the other end of the room to converse in peace.

Embarrassed, David began to sheaf through some sheet music.

"Sorry," Elizabeth whispered. He glanced at her askance, and she offered him an apologetic grin. "You're mortified, aren't you?"

He gave a small laugh. "A bit. Please don't take offence—" he added when he realised how that sounded. "I'm just not terribly at ease at social occasions."

"No offence taken," Elizabeth said, smiling. "It's a relief, actually. Father's juniors often feel obliged to be attentive to me. It's excruciating when you know someone's paying you compliments solely to please your father."

"I'm sure they pay you compliments for all sorts of reasons," David said in an awkward attempt to be gallant.

If anything, she looked even more sceptical. "Oh yes, I'm sure."

He realised she was suggesting that she was physically unappealing, and he wanted to tell her she was wrong. She wasn't beautiful, but he thought she looked a very pleasant sort of girl. He'd never want to bed her but not because of any deficiency in her person. It was entirely his own deficiency. He opened his mouth to say something reassuring but couldn't put his thoughts into an acceptable form of words. Instead he stared at her.

"Don't look so embarrassed, Mr. Lauriston." She laughed. "I count myself an excellent catch. It's just that sometimes I wish I was born beautiful."

Reassured, he blurted out a confession, hidden in an awkward burst of laughter. "Goodness, doesn't everyone?"

"Oh no, but you—" She halted, and there was a moment's awkwardness as David stared, helpless, at the flush that stained her cheeks scarlet.

He realised too late how rude he was being and tore his eyes away, looking down at the sheaf of sheet music in his hands. The top one was *Drink to Me Only with Thine Eyes*. "What about this one?" he asked, thrusting it under her nose.

She busied herself taking it from him and studying the music while her flush faded. "I think I could manage this one," she said at last. "It's nice and slow. Do you sing, Mr. Lauriston?"

David woke the next morning in one of the Jeffreys' guest bedchambers. It was small but charming, and the east-facing window drew in the morning sun. David had left the drapes open and now he basked in the warmth and brightness that flooded the room, stretching like a cat beneath the bedclothes. It felt luxurious. Between the reeky air and the high, crowded buildings of the Old Town, sunlight rarely penetrated his second-floor rooms.

He could tell from the quality of the light and the character of the birdsong that it was early. He wouldn't inconvenience Jeffrey's servants by getting up now and putting them to the bother of making his breakfast. Besides, it was pleasant to lie here, idle, no need to rise and dress and begin working.

Once the Chalmerses had left last night, Mrs. Jeffrey had begun quizzing him about Elizabeth. What was his impression of her? Did he not think her a very superior sort of girl? So clever and sensible. And her family connections would be most advantageous to him, didn't he think?

David had agreed but demurred that he could not possibly think to court a lady so far above him. Nonsense, declared both Mr. and Mrs. Jeffrey. David might not have much money yet, but Chalmers could help him build his reputation. And, Mrs. Jeffrey added, looking at him assessingly, her head to one side, he had so much else to offer. Jeffrey had laughed at that.

They swept aside all his protests and sketched out a glowing and very married future for him. It sounded perfect —or would to any other man in his position. How could he tell them he felt no attraction for women? That he had no intention of marrying?

He was not naïve. He knew that many men with his particular weakness married. He'd even toyed with the idea himself. It would be comfortable to have a wife and family. But always he came to the conclusion, he could not. The trouble was, he was his father's son. *"Honest to a fault,"* as his mother always complained. He couldn't bring himself to make oaths in church he knew he would be unable to keep. Sooner or later, he always lapsed. His weakness was like an aching tooth, always nagging.

The memory of his last lapse was still strong. Unforgettable, even. And right now it was making him hard, tempting him to indulge in solitary pleasures.

"I want you in my hand."

Sighing, he pushed the bedclothes down and his nightshirt up, exposing his rigid member to the chilly air. He took hold of himself.

"I want you in my mouth."

Slowly he stroked, revelling in the dragging pleasure. He closed his eyes and plundered his memory.

"I want to bury my tongue inside you —"

A dark wynd, a bulky body pressing into him, a firm hand tugging his bollocks, sharp teeth nipping his throat. Warm lips kissing the offence away.

"—and fuck you forever."

It felt like mere moments till he was coming, coating his belly in luscious pulses.

He lay staring at the ceiling for a long while afterwards, regret cooling his blood.

CHAPTER FIVE

Chalmers was as good as his word. Early the next week, he sought David out and asked him to work with him on a new case. The client, a Mr. MacAllister, had purchased lands in Fife so he could vote in a swiftly approaching election, but the local magistrates were refusing to enrol the man as a voter. The papers needed to be drafted straightaway. David had to set all his other work aside for several days and work late into the night on Wednesday.

He spent Thursday morning in the faculty library finalising his reading on the new case and the afternoon with Chalmers going through everything in fine detail. Chalmers called himself lazy, but a lazy man could not have acquired his seemingly fathomless knowledge of the law. He picked apart every sentence in the memorial David had prepared, challenging every assumption, demanding to be taken to the evidence for every assertion. David thanked God for the long hours he'd spent on the case. He withstood Chalmers's interrogation, though not without difficulty, and by the end of it, Chalmers was smiling.

"Good work, lad," he said, clapping David's shoulder. "We might even get this case lodged tomorrow. I'll speak to the solicitor in the morning." He gathered up the sheaf of papers David had given him and took his leave.

David sat for a moment, overcome with fatigue after his sleepless night. Eventually, he checked his watch, noting wearily that he needed to go if he was to be on time for his appointment with Euan MacLennan.

They were meeting in the Tolbooth Tavern, which had the dual attraction of being close to David's rooms on Blair Street and only a few minutes from the faculty library.

David's belly growled as he tidied the rest of his papers away, and he felt a little light-headed as he walked to the cloakroom to collect his greatcoat and hat. He hadn't eaten since breakfast, and even then he'd taken only toast and tea. His fingers shook slightly as he fastened his coat.

When he emerged from Parliament House, he saw that it had been raining. The cobblestones were slick, and fat drips of rainwater fell from the roof gutters. The last vestiges of the day's light were leeching out of the sky as he made his way down the High Street. It was late September now, and the nights were drawing in, a reminder that winter was on its way. Changes in the seasons seemed to creep up on him now that he lived in the city. Not like at home, on the farm, when every nuance of the weather and change in the hours of daylight were part of his working life.

This time of year always meant hard work at the farm. His father and Drew would have been run off their feet with harvesting over the last few weeks, and now they'd have a hundred and one things to do in preparation for winter: storing winter feed, carrying out repairs and doing any other jobs that needed attending to before the cold weather set in.

He should go and see his family soon. It had been months since his last visit, and there might be some big jobs his father could use another pair of hands on.

When he'd last seen them, months ago, in early summer, his father hadn't been well, and David had had to help Drew mend the barn roof. The weather had been kind, and when David had climbed down the ladder at suppertime, his face had been tight from a day spent in the sun. His body had ached all over too, though in the satisfying way that comes from a man using his body as God intended. It had been a hard day, but good. Companionable.

The aches David got from his daily work—from hunching over his desk and reading late into the night—were earned in a different way. These were physical manifestations of the work his mind did, even as his body atrophied at his desk. The stiffness in his neck and shoulders came from doing too little rather than too much.

Sometimes he needed to exhaust his body as well as his mind. But professional gentlemen did no labour, so when he felt the need for activity, David walked. Miles and miles. Most Saturdays he'd just shove some bread and cheese in his pocket and set off.

He wished he could do that now. Over the last two days, he'd worked to the point of mental exhaustion. Sleep would probably elude him tonight, despite his weariness. Thoughts of the new case still circled persistently in his mind. But it was too late to go walking, and anyway, he had to meet Euan. This short stroll down the High Street would have to do him for now.

The Tolbooth Tavern was quiet when he pushed the heavy wooden door open. Once his eyes had adjusted to the dim light, he saw that Euan was one of only three men drinking there.

The lad sat in front of the fire, his back to the door, steam rising from his wet coat as he nursed a small tankard.

"Hello," David said, taking off his hat and gesturing to the buxom woman behind the bar to bring more ale.

Euan turned in his seat, startled. "Davy! It's good to see you."

"Were you caught in the rain?" David asked as he settled himself down.

"Aye. Worse luck."

The woman arrived with the ale. She plonked a tankard on the table, displaying a large and pendulous cleavage. "Anythin' else, gents?"

David glanced at Euan questioningly. The younger man shook his head. David thought he looked too thin and worryingly pale.

"What do you have to eat?" David asked the woman.

"I could do you a bit of sausage and gravy."

"That'll do," David replied, without consulting Euan further. "Two plates."

The woman nodded and swayed back to the bar.

"I haven't got any money," Euan muttered once she'd moved away, his colour high.

"I'm paying."

"I don't want you to—"

"I'm paying." David's tone was final.

There was a brief silence. "Thank you," Euan said at last. "I need to find work. I've been looking."

"What about your studies?"

Euan fidgeted. "I can't keep them up without Peter's help," he admitted finally.

David stared at him. "You didn't mention this before. You said you were going back—"

"I can hardly go back if I have no funds, can I?"

"You can't give up on your studies! Your brother would be horrified."

Euan gave a mirthless laugh. "I don't have any choice. Anyway, that's the least of my worries. I'm more concerned about finding Lees."

David watched the young man for a moment, wrestling with himself. It was rare for men of their class to go to university, to move into the professions and achieve a better standard of living than that of the working families they'd come from. The thought of Euan giving up those aspirations after two years of study troubled David in ways he had difficulty putting into words. He thought of himself when he was a student, living in poverty, struggling to keep body and soul together but driven onwards by acquiring the education that he knew was the only way to change his life.

"I could help you with money," David said at last. His tone held more confidence than he truly felt—his finances were not good at the moment, but with Chalmers's sponsorship, there was every reason to think things would improve.

Euan shook his head, his cheeks red with humiliation. "I can make my own way in the world," he said.

"Everyone needs help sometimes."

"I thank you for your kindness, Davy, but I couldn't accept."

"Euan, I don't mind—"

"If you want to help me, all you need to do is try to find Lees." He paused before adding, "Have you managed to find anything out?"

Euan's pride was frustrating, but David knew he'd be the same in the lad's shoes, so he reluctantly acceded to Euan's change of subject and began to discuss the results of his enquiries.

"I have a few members of the faculty still to rule out," he concluded, "but so far, I've heard nothing to suggest there's any woman called Isabella with an advocate father."

"You don't think she's real, do you?"

David shrugged. "We both know that Lees could've been making her up as part of his story. Even if she's real, what he told Peter could be part truth and part lies. Her real name could be different."

Euan stared into the fire. "Peter said Lees was as drunk as a man can be and still able to talk. He was convinced Lees told him the truth that night." Euan glanced at David again, his gaze a little desperate. "That's all I have to go on."

"I'll keep looking into it," David assured him. "I've not completely eliminated the possibility that it's true. Not yet."

The barmaid arrived with their dinner then. The plates she set down on the table were made of tin and very old. Each plate held two fat sausages smothered in onions. Hunks of bread were already soaking up the thick brown gravy.

Euan waited until David began eating before he touched his own dinner, but once he started, he ate quickly, as though he was famished. He'd finished his whole plate by the time David had eaten just one of his sausages. Noticing this, David pushed his plate towards the other man.

"I ate earlier," he lied. "Do you want the rest of this?"

He feigned disinterest in Euan's answer, turning his attention to his ale and drinking deeply. There was a long, still pause, then the younger man drew the plate towards him and bent his head to eat again. He ate David's second sausage and meticulously scooped up all the onions and gravy with the bread. There wasn't a crumb on either plate when he was done.

The barmaid came to collect the plates while Euan was pissing outside.

"Another ale and a wee jug of whisky," David ordered, taking a purse of coins out of his coat pocket. "And I'll pay you now."

She named a sum, and he counted the coins into her hand; then she sailed away, her big bosom like the prow of a ship.

When Euan came back inside, he gave the fresh tankard waiting for him a troubled look. David knew if he met Euan's eyes, the lad would protest, so he ignored him, giving him time to settle. He concentrated on his own drink instead, filling the little dram glass the barmaid had brought him almost to the brim. When he raised it to his lips, he didn't drink immediately, just let the whisky lap at his mouth like a wave. The alcohol turned to vapour as soon as it touched him, alchemising into a cool breath of whisky on his lips. A wee kiss of it before he tipped the glass and let the first wet burn slide into his mouth and down his throat.

It was good, that feeling. He liked everything about it: the taste of the whisky, its fire. The way it numbed his over-wrought mind; the way it made him feel—after a while—more relaxed and expansive.

He should watch himself, though. He didn't feel as light-headed or hungry as when he'd left the library, but still, there wasn't much in his stomach. He'd be dead drunk after a few drams at this rate.

"Thank you for the food, Davy. And the ale."

"You're welcome." David smiled.

"I'll pay you back."

"No need."

"Nevertheless."

"Are you doing anything else to try to find Lees?" David asked, changing the subject. "Other than waiting to hear from me, I mean."

"I've been looking for him," Euan admitted. "I walk round the city every day. I'm getting to know Edinburgh well."

"You would recognise him, then?"

The young man nodded. "I used to go to meetings with Peter, till he made me stop. I met Lees a couple of times."

"So what does he look like?"

Euan leaned back in his seat and stared into the fire. "Tall. Dark haired. An English-sounding voice. He's got a funny way about him. Superior."

"You didn't like him," David surmised.

The other man turned his head and met David's questioning look with a serious gaze.

"Not a bit. I said so to Peter at the time."

David finished the jug of whisky in the same time it took Euan to finish his single tankard of ale. When he stood up to leave, the room reeled, then slowly came to rights. The reaction surprised him—he hadn't drunk *that* much—but the lack of food and sleep was telling on him now. He stumbled out of the tavern after Euan, wincing at the blast of cold air that hit them.

Euan pulled his cap over his ears. "When do you think you might learn more?" he asked.

"I can't be sure. Shall we meet again next week?"

"Where shall we meet?" Euan asked. He averted his eyes, his expression embarrassed. "To tell you the truth, I don't have the money to come to taverns and drink."

David resisted the urge to say he'd pay. The lad's pride had taken enough blows tonight. "Come to my rooms. I'm only round the corner from here, on Blair Street. Number twelve, on the second floor."

Euan nodded. "Number twelve, second floor. When shall I come? Monday?"

"Best leave it till Tuesday. Come in the evening. After seven would be best."

"All right. I don't know how to thank you, Davy."

"Just take care of yourself."

"I will. G'night."

"Good night."

With that, Euan turned and hurried away. He was swallowed into the shadows within seconds, as though he'd never been there.

David stood looking after him for a minute, wondering where the lad was sleeping; then he crammed his own hat on and set off on the short walk home.

The usual pockets of ne'er-do-wells, prostitutes and ragged children lurked in every doorway on the way, some eyeing him malevolently, others pleading for a coin or offering favours for one. One of them, a girl, ventured closer, brushing up against him. Her dress was pulled down to expose a meagre bosom and her feet were bare. She was either desperate for a client or trying to steal something, her fingers whispering over the placket of his breeches. Her dead, calculating expression filled him with pity even as he pushed her firmly away.

At last he was home and trudging up the stone stairs of the close. He unlocked his front door and went inside, carefully locking up behind him. Going straight to the kitchen, he checked the larder. It was fairly bare, as usual. His stomach was gnawing with hunger, though, and he reached for the easiest thing to eat, a bit of cheese that was past its best. Paring away the rind, he ate it where he stood, then went to get ready for bed.

That night, he dreamed about William for the first time in years.

He was in the kirk at Midlauder, sitting in his family's pew, except instead of his mother and father and Drew, it was William sitting next to him. Even though, in real life, William had always sat in the front pew with his father, Sir Thomas Lennox, and all the pretty Lennox girls. The most David had ever seen of William in church was the back of his head.

In the dream, though, William was sitting next to him, and, instead of his Sunday clothes, he was wearing a loose shirt and old breeches and had bare feet.

"Let's go swimming, Davy," he said, and his eyes gleamed with excitement. Eyes the same yellowy-green as the mossy bark on the old beech tree they liked to climb. There was a thick branch you could stand on and jump off, into the pond.

"I can't, I'm in my Sunday clothes," David said.

"No you're not."

He looked down, and no, he wasn't. He was in his court gown. He put his hand to his head—he was wearing his court wig too. He drew it off, feeling silly. He was a man, then, not a boy.

And so, he realised, was William.

The open neck of William's shirt displayed a swathe of

pale skin dusted with dark hair. His shoulders were broad and powerful, his thighs muscled from riding. He smiled at David, and his smile was inviting.

"William—" His stomach churned with excitement and shame. He wanted William the way a man wants a woman, and it was so very wrong to feel this way. Especially about his friend.

William didn't say anything. He just reached for David's breeches, unfastening the buttons and freeing his aching cock, then bending over to—Christ, was he going to put it in his mouth?

Helplessly, David reached for William's head, wanting to guide him to his quarry. But then it all became farcical, silly. He couldn't get hold of William, kept bucking his hips in a fruitless search for a warm, wet mouth that was proving to be completely elusive. He was almost weeping with frustration by the time he woke up, his limbs snarled in the bed sheets.

He lay, shaken, staring at the ceiling.

He hadn't thought of William in a long time—until this business with Euan. Now, in the depths of night, he found himself remembering the very last time he'd seen his friend, leaving Midlauder in his father's carriage, bound for Oxford. David had been working in one of his father's fields when the carriage had rumbled slowly past. He'd glimpsed William looking out of the carriage window and had run to the road, waving madly, getting there just in time to see the carriage disappearing into the distance.

That last glimpse had been fleeting. The time before had been a week earlier. That was the day David's father had almost disowned him. Because of a kiss.

The dream version of William might try to take David's cock in his mouth, but the real William never had. There had never been anything like that between them, no matter what David's father might have thought. Just a handful of kisses.

58

Three to be precise. Three heart-thundering, soul-stealing kisses.

David knew it was wrong to get down on his knees and take a man's cock in his mouth. He lived with the torment that visited him every time he succumbed to his weakness. Those kisses with William were different, though. David had never been able to truly reconcile himself to what his father had said to him the day he'd caught them—that their kiss was evil in God's eyes.

He'd pleaded with his father to understand. He and William were loving friends, like David and Jonathan in the Bible. But his father had just become more and more enraged until finally he'd cracked and knocked David to the ground with a punch from one of his work-hardened fists.

The love David had felt for William all those years ago had been pure, untainted by the lust that troubled his dreams now.

As he lay there in the dark, sleepless in his lonely bed, David wished he could recapture that feeling. If only for one hour.

CHAPTER SIX

"You'd better stay for dinner."

It wasn't so much an invitation as an order, though Chalmers was smiling as he leaned back in his chair. They'd been working in Chalmers's study all day, honing the argument for the first hearing of Mr. MacAllister's case tomorrow. The clock on the mantelpiece had just chimed six.

"Mrs. Chalmers has invited some young gentleman visiting from London for dinner," the older man continued. "I think she's got Elizabeth married off to him already, in her own head."

"In that case, I shouldn't intrude," David said as he tied up his papers in a loose bundle.

"Nonsense. It'll be no trouble to lay another place for you, and it always does to have more than one eligible gentleman at the table when there are four young ladies."

"I'm hardly eligible," David scoffed.

"You're alive, aren't you?" Chalmers said drily. "Besides, you'll be eligible in time. Maybe you'll end up occupying some great baronial pile like our friend Mr. Jeffrey."

David laughed. Jeffrey was an original, and his choice of home reflected that. Chalmers, however, was more typical of their profession. He lived in the New Town, in a terraced townhouse, right at the end of a long, curving crescent. It was precisely the sort of house that David hoped to live in one day. And who would not? Who would not prefer the elegantly mathematical symmetry of the New Town to the tumbledown filth and clutter of the Old Town? No wonder Chalmers had asked David to come to his house to work on the case rather than travelling in to the Lawnmarket, where he'd have to push his way through hordes of hawkers and beggars and prostitutes before he even reached the faculty library.

Chalmers gave a yawn, peeling off his spectacles and scrubbing his hands over his face as David packed up his papers.

"Well, we've done a good day's work," he said, rising from his seat at the desk they'd shared all day. "And I, for one, don't intend to give it another thought before tomorrow's hearing. Let's have a drink."

David smiled at how unfazed Chalmers was at the prospect of tomorrow's hearing. If David were doing the speaking, he'd have spent the whole evening going over his submissions again. But his role tomorrow would be limited to listening and note-taking.

Chalmers crossed the room, walking past a full wall lined with books. Legal treatises, historical monographs, philosophical works. The man, David had discovered, was a bibliophile. But for now, Chalmers was happy to ignore his books, stopping in front of a cabinet in the corner of the room which, once opened, revealed several decanters. He withdrew one, half full of amber liquor.

"Water of Life," Chalmers said, smiling. "Would you like a dram, lad?"

He was pulling out the glasses already. David's acquiescence was a formality, but he gave it anyway.

"All right, then."

The measure Chalmers poured was generous and the quality of the whisky was excellent, the taste smoky on David's tongue.

"It's from Islay," Chalmers said. "Do you like it?"

David nodded. "That's a rare malt." He swallowed the last bit and put the glass down on the polished wood.

"Have another."

David gave in to temptation. "Just one more, then, thank you."

After the second, there were two more. Chalmers poured them without asking, and David drank them while they chattered about faculty matters.

"You might be wee," Chalmers said, after a while, "but you can certainly put the whisky away. If I'd just walked in here, I'd never guess a drop had passed your lips."

"I'm not wee," David said with a smile he had to force. "I'm five feet and seven inches." It was a good height, though it was true that he was slender and often assumed to be shorter as a result.

"Are you? You look like a gust of wind could blow you over."

David hid his irritation at that comment. "I'm stronger than I look."

Chalmers smiled affably. "I don't doubt it, lad. Come on, let's go down. It'll be dinnertime soon."

"I really should go," David demurred. "Mrs. Chalmers will be inconvenienced by an extra guest."

Chalmers shook his head. "Put that thought out of your mind, lad. You're staying."

When they went down to the drawing room it was to find Mrs. Chalmers, Elizabeth and her sisters gathered there in apparent domestic harmony. The girls all sat with their hands folded primly in their laps, while Mrs. Chalmers embroidered. They all looked up when the two men entered the room, disappointment registering on all but one of their faces to see their father and David. Only Elizabeth smiled, her eyes wide with surprise.

"Good evening, Mr. Lauriston," she said. "How nice to see you again." Her mother gave her a sharp look.

"I've invited Mr. Lauriston to join us for dinner," Chalmers announced to the room. Mrs. Chalmers's jaw tightened speakingly, but she merely nodded and rose from her chair.

"Excuse me," she said. "I must speak with Cook and the servants. The table will have to be entirely rearranged."

"Oh, please don't—" David began, but Chalmers cut him off.

"Thank you, my dear," he said to his departing spouse and ushered David farther into the room. "Come and meet my girls, Lauriston."

David bowed to the three daughters he hadn't yet met, Maria, Catherine and Jane, before he turned to Elizabeth.

"And Miss Elizabeth," he said. "How nice to see you again."

"Mr. Lauriston," she replied, smiling widely. "I hear you're working with Father on one of his cases. I'm delighted you could join us this evening. It is a most unexpected pleasure to see you again."

"The delight is all mine," David said gallantly, enjoying the way her face became brighter and more attractive as they conversed. She was an unremarkable-looking girl when she was silent, but when she spoke, her face was transformed. He couldn't remember ever seeing someone so expressive.

"Has Father told you we have another gentleman joining us this evening?" Her dark eyes twinkled with merriment. "He is the younger son of a marquess, no less! We are all terribly excited to be meeting such a grand personage."

"So I have heard," David said, lips twitching. Plainly, whatever her mother thought, Elizabeth was not overawed at the thought of dining with a peer of the realm.

At that moment, the man they were speaking of arrived.

The footman entered first. "Lord Murdo Balfour, sir," he said, addressing Mr. Chalmers.

David thought stupidly, *I know that name.* For the briefest instant, he didn't connect it with the man at whose feet he'd knelt.

And then he saw him.

Murdo Balfour stood behind the footman, tall, broad-shouldered and expensively dressed. Familiar, yet not.

All of David's ease left him, leeching away as his gut began to churn and his breath constricted in his throat. As their gazes met and held.

Yes, it was him. The man from the inn at Stirling. The man who'd stroked David's cock in a filthy alleyway; whose own cock David had got down on his knees to suck.

He gave no sign of recognising David, but somehow David was sure he did, and then his gaze was moving on, honing in on Mr. Chalmers who was moving forward to greet him.

"Lord Murdo," Chalmers said, offering his hand. "Welcome to my home."

"Mr. Chalmers, I presume. I'm very pleased to meet you, sir."

"My wife has been detained a moment. She will be back in a—"

"Good heavens, Lord Murdo! How mortifying that I wasn't here to greet you!" Mrs. Chalmers bustled into the room, her voice high and excited, her colour up. "So good of you to come! You have met my husband?"

Balfour smiled at her. "We have introduced ourselves, Mrs. Chalmers. How nice to see you again."

Mrs. Chalmers gave an oddly girlish titter. "Well, then, I only need to introduce you to our daughters, my lord. They are all very excited to meet you."

"Don't forget Mr. Lauriston, Mother," Elizabeth said,

earning herself a maternal frown. She wasn't to know that David was only too happy to linger in the background.

Good God, the man was a *lord*. The younger son of a marquess. He hadn't divulged that nugget at the inn in Stirling.

Balfour's attention wandered back to David, despite being surrounded by the Chalmers girls—yes, he knew who David was all right. Their gazes met over one of the younger girl's heads, and David couldn't look away. His attention was snagged, like cloth catching on a nail.

It was only for a moment, but it felt like forever that they stared at each other. As for Balfour, he didn't smile as such, but there was something in his face. Something still and knowing, though he was the first to look away.

Eventually it was David's turn to be introduced to the guest of honour.

"And this is Mr. Lauriston," Mrs. Chalmers said in her most chilly voice as she approached him, Balfour at her side. "He's working on a case with Mr. Chalmers at present." She paused, then added grudgingly, "Mr. Lauriston, Lord Murdo Balfour."

Balfour put out his hand, the hint of a smile playing over his well-shaped lips. "I'm pleased to meet you, Mr. Lauriston."

His hand was steady. His voice likewise, the warm depth of it caressing, that English-sounding accent smooth and mellifluous, so foreign compared to the clipped cadence of everyone else in the room.

David forced his own hand out. "And I you, my lord." Balfour's grip was warm, firm.

As David drew away, he thought that Balfour—he couldn't think of him by any other name—gave his hand the lightest press. But the man's expression remained so politely distant that afterwards David wondered if he'd imagined it.

After that, Balfour was swallowed up by the females in

the party again, particularly the three younger ladies. They peppered him with questions about his life in London and his journey north, while David stood quietly by and watched.

When they went in to dinner, David discovered that he'd been sandwiched between the two youngest daughters, Maria and Jane. The older girls had pride of place on either side of Balfour.

The meal felt interminable. David had enjoyed Elizabeth's company at Jeffrey's house but Maria and Jane had no interest in anything other than gowns and hair ribbons and who had danced with who at some assembly they'd attended the previous week. David sat, morosely silent, and soon they cut him out of the conversation altogether, simply leaning past him to talk to each other, while he tried to listen to the others at the table.

"I gather your father's estate is in Argyllshire, my lord," Mrs. Chalmers said to Balfour. "It is so far from here! May I ask what has drawn you to Edinburgh?"

Balfour smiled. "I have some friends here, ma'am. But the chief reason for my visit is to see the fair city itself." He paused and looked round the table at the ladies. "I think I have been lucky to see some of its beauty here this evening."

Mrs. Chalmers tittered. "You are very kind."

Chalmers spoke then. "You have friends in Edinburgh, my lord?" he asked politely.

"Yes, sir. As your lady wife already knows, we have a connection in common. Sir Edward Galbraith is a long-standing friend of my father."

Chalmers looked more interested at this. "You know Sir Edward, do you? We were on opposite sides of many cases. A fine opponent, he was. A shame he gave the law up. He was a very fine advocate."

Balfour smiled. "He has put his debating talents to good use in Parliament, though. My father and his friends are glad of his skills as an orator."

"I daresay," Chalmers replied. "He always was a persuasive fellow. Your father is in politics, then?"

Balfour waved his hand. "He holds some small office in government." A careless smile. "I can never remember the title. Politics doesn't interest me, I'm afraid."

"Not everyone cares for matters of State, it's true," Chalmers replied in a neutral tone, before returning his attention to his roast pigeon.

"Sir Edward's daughter and I went to the same ladies' seminary," Elizabeth interjected.

Balfour turned to Elizabeth, a look of polite interest on his face.

"Bella and I are great friends," Elizabeth continued. "She and her mother spend most of the year in Scotland. Lady Galbraith detests London, so we see each other a good deal. They live on Heriot Row, which is only a few minutes' walk away."

Bella?

Balfour smiled at Elizabeth. "I am well acquainted with Miss Galbraith and her mother," he said. "And I shall be calling on them at the earliest opportunity."

Lees got drunk with Peter and told him about a young woman called Isabella. She lives here in Edinburgh.

When Euan had described Lees, it had occurred to David that his description—*tall, dark-haired, an English-sounding voice* —sounded rather like the man he'd sucked off in an alleyway in Stirling. But it hadn't been more than a passing thought. Why would it be? Many men looked like that. Now, though, with the mention of this girl, Bella, whose father had once been an advocate, the thought of Lees loomed large, and David found himself glancing at Balfour again through new eyes.

"On Saturday evening, Catherine and I are attending the assembly in town with Bella. Do you intend to go, my lord?"

Elizabeth directed the question to Balfour, but her eyes flickered towards David.

"I should certainly like to do so," Balfour said. "And I will hope to dance with you, Miss Chalmers."

Mrs. Chalmers, who had begun to look a little unhappy at the direction the conversation had taken, looked mollified at this particular attention to her oldest daughter, while Elizabeth blushed and glanced again at David, an odd, pained expression in her eyes. Puzzled, David smiled at her, and she seemed to brighten.

When he looked away from Elizabeth, it was to discover Balfour's gaze on him, cool and assessing. He averted his eyes, reaching for his wineglass and hoping no one had noticed the warmth he'd felt steal over his cheeks.

At last the meal was over, and the ladies withdrew to take tea while Chalmers brought out the whisky again.

David had had several glasses of wine at dinner and, of course, all those drams in Chalmers's study. He knew he should stop drinking. He felt the telltale signs of his self-control loosening. His mind had begun to fixate on that night in Stirling, his gaze creeping again and again to Balfour, lingering on his broad, black-clad shoulders and the snowy linen wound round his throat. He knew himself in dangerous territory and dug his fingers into his palms to stop his hands stealing out to pick up the glass. Even as he resisted, though, another part of his mind urged him to drink. What did it matter, after all? What was the worst that could happen? The whisky would relax him, and God knew he was wound as tight as a spring.

He tried to concentrate on the conversation between the other two men to distract himself. Chalmers was quizzing Balfour about the unsuccessful plot to murder the Prime Minister and his Cabinet earlier in the year.

"It is said that Lord Liverpool can hardly venture outside for fear of attack," the older man observed.

Balfour shrugged. "Radicals," he said shortly. "They are few but fanatical."

Chalmers smiled. "You do realise you are in the company of someone who defended some radicals?"

Balfour looked briefly surprised. "You defended the weavers?"

"Not I," Chalmers said. "Mr. Lauriston was their champion."

Balfour's head swung round, dark eyes penetrating, a question in his raised brows.

"I worked with Mr. Jeffrey on the defence of two of the weavers who were executed," David said shortly, unwilling to share more than that.

Balfour stared. "I see," he said after a long pause.

There was a brief, uncomfortable silence.

"Tell me, my lord, is London your permanent home?" Chalmers smoothed over the odd, tense moment with a bland question.

"For most of the year," Balfour replied, turning his attention to the older man. "I try to come up to Kilbeigh—my father's estate—at least once a year. I usually come in spring or autumn, as I prefer to avoid the place when the midges are biting."

Chalmers laughed. "Oh, I am all too familiar with those beasties! They are at their worst in the west, are they not?"

"You are from the west, then? Rather than Edinburgh?"

Chalmers nodded. "I hail from Oban, originally. Though I've lived here for thirty-two years now and count myself almost a native."

That accounted for the faint lilt in Chalmers's voice, then.

"Do you ever see yourself returning home?" Balfour asked.

"Goodness, no! I would miss city life. I like my club. I dine there twice a week at least. And I enjoy the debates at the Speculative Society of which I am a member. My friends are all faculty men, like me. I should miss their company greatly if I moved away."

David suppressed a smile. It did not escape him that Chalmers's favourite occupations all kept him away from his shrewish wife.

"You prefer the intellectual life," Balfour observed.

"Infinitely," Chalmers agreed. "And you, my lord? Will you ever exchange the pleasures of London for those of the country?"

"Actually, I am considering just that."

"Really?"

"Yes, I've been looking for a property for some time. Kilbeigh will go to my older brother, of course."

"What kind of property do you seek?" David asked.

Balfour turned his head to meet David's curious gaze. "Something in the country. To begin with I was determined it should be small." He gave a lazy smile. "A mere cottage, if you can believe it, Mr. Lauriston."

David raised a brow. "I doubt my idea of a cottage is the same as yours, my lord."

Balfour's dark eyes twinkled and the corner of his mouth lifted, that dimple of his flashing for the first time this evening.

"Perhaps not," he conceded. "I was originally thinking of a hunting lodge. Somewhere I could put up a few guests with decent fishing."

"Hardly a cottage," David observed, smiling to take the sting out of the comment.

"True. In any event, as it happens, I've taken a liking for a property in Perthshire that's rather larger than a lodge and most impractical. It's far too big for me and was left in a muddle by the last owner, whose executors have been trying to get rid of it for more than a twelvemonth."

Chalmers chuckled. "It sounds like a bad bargain, my lord. Stay away, that's my advice."

"What do you like about it?" David asked.

The other corner of Balfour's mouth lifted. He had beautifully carved lips for a man, the upper bow very precisely symmetrical, the philtrum above a deep, sensual groove. When he smiled, as he was doing now, that appealing little pleat of flesh flattened and stretched, and that unexpected dimple appeared in his left cheek. David blinked and looked down at the tablecloth.

"The views are exquisite," Balfour said. "Very romantic."

Chalmers laughed outright then. "Romantic views? Oh beware! Beware! Many a bad bargain has been made over a romantic view. Marriages have crumbled and fortunes been lost. Take my word for it. Stay away."

"I'm sure you're right," Balfour replied with a chuckle. "I'll try to rein in my poetic soul."

"You do that," Chalmers said. "In the meantime, have another whisky. There's enough poetry in this bottle for any man's soul."

It was only then, as Chalmers refilled their glasses, that David realised he'd drunk the last dram without even noticing.

"It's a good whisky," Balfour agreed, holding his glass up to the candlelight.

"You like whisky?" Chalmers asked.

"Yes, though I prefer French brandy generally," he replied, adding with a grin, "smuggled, of course."

"They don't look dissimilar in the glass. Until you taste them," Chalmers observed.

"And yet they have such different ingredients," Balfour said.

"The colour doesn't come from the ingredients," David interjected quietly. "It comes from the wood barrels the spirit's stored in."

"Goodness me, Mr. Lauriston," Balfour drawled. "What a thing to know! You are not just a pretty face, are you?"

David's cheeks heated again. Christ, he wished he could control his blushes.

"Oh, our Mr. Lauriston is bright, all right," Chalmers said, chuckling. "I'm fortunate enough to get more briefs than I can manage alone, so I employ junior advocates to work with me. But they have to be the very best, you see. Not the ten-a-penny ones with dull minds and aristocratic families. I don't need more influence with the judges—I've got that in spades already. No, I want a man with *intellect*. Like this young man."

Balfour listened to Chalmers's soliloquy with fascination. "You rate him highly."

"I do indeed," Chalmers replied jovially. The whisky was making him fulsome in his praise. He reached for the bottle to pour himself another.

Balfour transferred his attention to David, his gaze strangely assessing. He did nothing to veil his interest, and it made his scrutiny feel almost painfully intimate, invasive even. It put David's back up, and before he knew what he was doing, he was on his feet, the chair scraping against the floor with a shriek. Chalmers looked up, surprised. Balfour merely raised his eyebrows.

"I should be going," David finally got out, astonished by how ordinary his voice sounded. "Before all these compliments turn my head."

Chalmers laughed. "You should enjoy them while you can, lad," he said. "Are you sure you won't stay for a last dram?"

"No, I should be on my way. Tomorrow is going to be demanding."

"You're right, of course." Chalmers sighed. "And we have an early start." He rang the bell. Moments later, the footman entered and Chalmers dispatched him for David's greatcoat and hat.

"Leave your papers. I'll bring them in with me tomorrow,"

Chalmers said. "And don't think of reading anything more tonight. I know exactly what I'm going to be saying."

David nodded. He felt Balfour's gaze on him, heavy and warm, but didn't look at him as he donned his coat. And so he was unaware, until he turned around, that Balfour was also readying himself to leave.

"You are welcome to stay, my lord," Chalmers told Balfour as the footman left the room. "Mr. Lauriston wishes to leave because he has important work to do tomorrow, but I fancy you do not."

If there was a fragment of sarcasm in there, Balfour didn't appear to notice. "Forgive me for taking my leave so early, but I'm terribly tired," he replied. "It was a long journey from Argyll, and I've only just arrived. Please pass my apologies on to your lady."

Mrs. Chalmers would be annoyed. She'd have the girls all arranged in the drawing room, ready to show off their accomplishments, Elizabeth likely at the pianoforte. But though Chalmers must know this, he merely inclined his head. "I hope you will call on us again, my lord."

"I will do so gladly," Balfour replied, accepting his coat and sliding his arms into the sleeves. "And thank you for a most pleasant evening."

He turned to David. "Shall we walk together, Lauriston?"

CHAPTER SEVEN

Outside, it was dark and foggy. The few oil lamps attached to the houses on the street sent out feeble rings of light, but not enough to illuminate the road ahead. Balfour loomed large at David's side, his face shadowed by the brim of his high-crowned hat.

His presence unsettled David. He wished the man had had the courtesy to stay at Chalmers's house a little longer, but Balfour had seemed to welcome the opportunity to escape early.

"Where do you live, Lauriston?"

"In the Old Town," David replied shortly.

"How far is that on foot?"

"Not far. A walk of twenty minutes, perhaps. And you?"

"My townhouse is on Queen Street, so you will have my company at least part of the way home."

David noted the wealthy address without comment and set off, Balfour falling into step beside him.

"I didn't expect to see someone I knew tonight," Balfour said after a while. It was his first acknowledgement that he remembered David.

David glanced at him. The detail of Balfour's face was

difficult to make out in the darkness, but the strong, certain lines of his profile were oddly familiar. "Nor did I," he said quietly.

Balfour turned to look at him and laughed, his wide, white grin flashing in the shadows. "Was it a shock?"

David couldn't help but smile back. There was something infectious about Balfour's grin. "A bit of one," he admitted, thawing a little.

"Particularly when you're trying to court the oldest daughter of the house, I imagine."

David stumbled. "I beg your pardon?"

"The daughter—Elizabeth, was it? She's sweet on you. And Chalmers approves, though his lady is aiming higher, I gather." He clapped David on the shoulder. "Don't worry, you'll have no competition from me, whatever your future mother-in-law might hope. I have my eye on another lady."

David stopped in his tracks, his brows drawing together. "I am not courting Miss Chalmers."

Balfour halted beside him, seeming surprised at David's emphatic tone. "All right," he said. "Have it your way. Though if you have any sense, that's what you'll do. It'd be an advantageous match for a man of your station." He grinned again, allowing his gaze to travel over David in a slow, head-to-toe examination. "And there'd be compensations for the lady."

David pressed his lips together as they recommenced walking, annoyed beyond all reason. Not even sure why he was annoyed.

"What do you mean, a man of my station?"

Balfour turned his head to look at him, and David had the disconcerting feeling that Balfour saw everything David was thinking, while Balfour remained entirely opaque to him, hidden in the shadows.

"Well, you don't come from money, do you?" Balfour said.

"No," David admitted. "I don't."

"I'm guessing that you can't afford to fail at your profession. You don't have wealth to fall back on. And you probably don't have connections with influence. In all likelihood, you've had to fight to get to where you are now, and even now, you're standing on the bottom rung of the ladder. Am I right?"

David swallowed, not liking the feeling of being so sharply observed. "You're not wrong," he admitted stiffly.

Balfour smiled. "You look and sound the part, Lauriston, and you're plainly intelligent. But there are a few clues here and there—in your speech, your dress, your gestures. Most especially those, actually." He paused. "Marriage to a woman like Elizabeth Chalmers would help you greatly. And it's well within your reach."

Stung by Balfour's thorough assessment, David blurted, "I would never consider it."

Balfour shrugged. "Well, you should."

"But I could not love her."

Balfour regarded him thoughtfully. "Are you a romantic, I wonder," he said. "Or an idealist?" He canted his head to one side, as though debating the point, then seemed to reach a decision. "Both, possibly."

"I'm neither. But I imagine most women expect love when they marry. And that is something that I—" He broke off for a moment, then determinedly resumed. "That I, with my unnatural defect, am unable to give."

Balfour just stared at him. David held himself still under the astonished examination, determined not to squirm, even though he felt like an insect on a pin.

"Yes, definitely an idealist," Balfour murmured. "Only an idealist could believe most women expect love when they marry. They're very practical creatures, you know. And as for your talk about unnatural defects, must you speak like some fire-and-brimstone preacher? I suppose you were brought up to believe it's the worst sin in Christendom?"

He sounded so scathing that heat invaded David's face. "Yes, I was brought up to believe it's a sin. Not to mention a crime. It's not something I'm proud of. Are you?"

Balfour laughed. "Proud of it? I don't even think about it in those terms. I don't think the fact I want to stick my cock in the occasional arse is any business of God, the King or anyone else. I'm not harming anyone when I bugger a pretty boy— assuming the pretty boy is of age and willing. And I'm not going to flagellate myself with regret over something that brings me a great deal of pleasure. Does that answer your question?"

"Perfectly." Face burning, David turned on his heel and began to walk away, mortification crawling over his skin. The man was an unapologetic reprobate and plainly he thought David was a stiff-necked bore.

"Hold up there!" Balfour called after him, laughter still in his deep voice. "Are you offended, Lauriston?"

"Not a bit," David said tersely.

"Yes, you are. You think I'm an ungodly villain, when the truth is I'm a slave to reason."

"A slave to reason?" David scoffed.

"Quite so. I've never been able to accept that things are a certain way just because someone tells me they are. I don't believe that fucking a man is a mortal sin. It harms no one, and it brings a great deal of pleasure to me."

"That must be convenient."

Balfour laughed again, as though pleased by David's dry comment. "It is. But it's also true, I think. I am the sovereign of this." He gestured to his own body. "And I will do with it what I will."

"And what about this lady you have your eye on? What if you marry her?"

"What of it?"

"You will be giving yourself to her, and she will be giving

77

herself to you. You won't be sole sovereign of your body then."

Balfour frowned and smiled at the same time, a strange combination of expressions that made him look puzzled and good humoured at once. "You're serious."

"Yes, I'm serious," David replied. "Even if you don't believe what the Bible says, when you marry, you make promises. Marriage vows."

"Are you quite sure you're a lawyer, Lauriston? There is something touchingly naïve about you at times that is quite at odds with your profession."

David flushed again. "I realise you think I'm ridiculous, but a man of honour would not laugh at me."

"Are you calling me dishonourable?" Balfour's voice was disbelieving, a dangerous edge creeping in.

David refused to back down. "Would you make promises to a woman in church, then break those promises? Is that not dishonourable?"

"It is the way of the world. Like as not any woman I marry won't expect—or want—my fidelity."

"It doesn't matter what she expects or wants," David said implacably. "A promise is a promise."

Balfour gave a disbelieving laugh. "You *are* an idealist."

David thought about that. "Perhaps," he conceded at last. "And glad to be one if only an idealist keeps his promises."

Balfour didn't answer that, but he looked at David for a long moment before he turned his head forward again.

"Why did you represent those weavers?"

The unexpectedness of the question after the brief silence threw David. "Because they deserved to be properly defended."

"Because they were right?"

"Because anyone in their position deserves to be represented by an advocate who will try his best for them."

"Avoiding the question, Lauriston?"

"No. Answering it honestly. That is the reason I represented them. If you want to know if I agree with their views, you need to ask me another question."

"Do you agree with their views?"

"Do you?"

Balfour laughed, though not humorously this time. He turned his head, his eyes travelling over David's face. There was something heated and intense in his gaze that made David's gut clench. "You first."

David shrugged, cultivating a cool expression even as he suppressed the dangerous glimmer of attraction. "Some of them. I believe the suffrage should be extended. I think if it is not, there will be much more violence. Perhaps even a people's revolution, as happened in France."

"And would you welcome war between the classes?"

"Of course not."

"But your weavers would have done so. They went to war, did they not? A short-lived war, but a war nonetheless." The deep voice was all seriousness now.

David stared at Balfour, fear and attraction churning inside him, an unpleasant combination that nevertheless made him feel fully alive in a way he hadn't felt in a long time. Was this man Lees? He was not speaking tonight like a man nourishing a secret passion for a woman, but he knew Isabella Galbraith all right. She might be the lady he had his eye on. And he fitted Lees's description. He could be the man Euan MacLennan sought.

"The weavers told me that the war, if you can call those skirmishes a war, happened because of government agents. Men they believed to be their own, who deliberately provoked those events with the sole purpose of flushing out those most likely to speak out against the government."

Balfour met his gaze. "Is that so? Who were these agents, Lauriston? What happened to them?"

They faced each other on the cold, dark street, the mist snaking between them.

"I should dearly like to know," David said. "People died because of those men."

"Perhaps people were saved because of them."

"We'll never know, will we? Their actions deprived the weavers of the chance to decide for themselves how they would act. Perhaps they would never have raised arms against the government. Now three of those men are dead and the rest are being transported. Not to mention the people killed in the riots."

"And look how many died by the guillotine in France," Balfour said. "Would that be better?"

"If France teaches us anything, it is that it's unwise to crush the people."

For a moment there was a heavy silence between them, pregnant with turmoil. David's heart thudded in his chest. Then Balfour shrugged and began to walk again. "In truth, I do not disagree with you on that."

Surprised by Balfour's sudden concession, David fell into step beside him, gradually calming, and for a while, they merely walked, David still wondering if Balfour was Lees, and, if he was, what he thought of the result of his actions.

When they turned onto Queen Street, Balfour said, "My house is halfway along."

The oil lamps in this part of town were more numerous than on the smaller streets, but even so, the light was poor. Nevertheless, when David glanced at Balfour, he was able to tell somehow that the other man was preoccupied. Was it that David's eyes had grown more used to the dark by now? Or was it something else, more ephemeral and intuitive?

Strange, the clues to a man's soul. The pitch of Balfour's hunched shoulders was expressive. Something about his fixed gaze suggested he was looking inward. David turned his own gaze away, giving the man his privacy and retreating into his own thoughts.

Soon enough, they were stopping in front of a tall, thin, grand house, part of a row of tall, thin, grand houses.

"Here we are," Balfour said, turning to David and giving him a very direct look. "Would you like to come in?"

Although the prospect of such an invitation had crossed David's mind, he felt a measure of surprise. They had done nothing but argue since they'd left Chalmers's house, and he rather thought Balfour might've decided against extending the evening. As for David, whilst the thought of that night in Stirling had been haunting him ever since, he knew it would be very unwise to seek to reenact it. He made sure never to go with the same man twice, keeping his encounters as anonymous as possible.

And then there was the fact that it seemed Balfour might have some connection to the mysterious Lees.

"I think not," David said at last, quietly.

"Are you sure?" Balfour said, stepping closer, his voice deep and intimate. "I enjoyed our last time together. I would like to do it again. Wouldn't you?"

His body brushed against David's, and David felt as though his whole being had come to life just from that light touch.

Yes, he wanted to do it again. He wanted it more than anything. But that didn't make it right, and dear God, the man might be *Lees*, responsible for the transportation of Peter MacLennan amongst others, and the deaths of good men.

And wouldn't it be best to find out for sure? an insidious little voice said inside him. *You can't just walk away now. Go with him.*

But of course, Balfour being the direct, unsettling man that he was, offered no pretext for the invitation. If he'd asked David in to drink or talk, David could've accepted and told himself it was only polite or that he sought more knowledge of the man. He could've allowed the inevitable to happen in manageable increments. But no, Murdo Balfour did not dissemble. He simply told David he wanted him and made him choose.

"I would like to do it again. Wouldn't you?"

There was no going in that house for any other purpose, or even pretending to do so.

David imagined Balfour's cock in his mouth, how it would feel to rub his face against the hard, hot flesh and engulf it in his own willing throat. He was hard now, and as the idea took hold of his mind, one of Balfour's hands pressed against the placket of his breeches, roughly caressing his erection.

"I want you in my mouth this time," Balfour said raggedly. "And I want to fuck you."

The first statement felt like a caress. The second, like a splash of cold water in his face. David didn't allow himself to be fucked. Ever. It was one thing to suck a cock, quite another to let a man penetrate his body. Hypocritical, perhaps, but he needed to maintain some moral fences if he wasn't to go mad.

"Better not," he said finally, stepping back and adding truthfully, "I have court tomorrow morning."

Balfour dropped his hand. He said nothing, his dark eyes searching David's face, and though David tried to present a calm, indifferent expression, he could tell from the way Balfour watched him that he saw something of David's turmoil.

"Very well," he said at last with a sardonic twist of his lips. "As I said, I prefer my pretty boys willing."

He began to turn away, but David shot out a hand, grabbing him by the elbow, detaining him. "I'm not pretty," he gritted out. "Or a boy, for that matter. I'm four and twenty."

Balfour gave him a long look. "You're a boy all right," he sneered. "An idealistic, romantic, pretty boy. It's why your Miss Chalmers is so enamoured with you. Because you're beautiful, virtuous and utterly unthreatening." He shook off David's hand. "But that doesn't interest me, Mr. Lauriston. I don't want someone who practically faints when I tell him I want to fuck him. I want someone who knows how to give pleasure and receive it too. So go home, back to your monkish bed, and flagellate yourself for wanting something—someone —you're not supposed to want. I can easily find someone else just as pretty as you and a great deal more willing."

Having delivered this speech, Balfour turned on his heel and marched up the steps to rap at the door of his house with his cane. A few moments later, the door creaked open, revealing a footman holding a candle.

Shocked into stillness by Balfour's verbal assassination, David remained where he stood and watched as Balfour strode into his house without so much as a backward glance.

Only when the footman closed the door did he finally move again, turning towards the Old Town and home.

CHAPTER EIGHT

The following day was busy, and it was late when David got home.

The hearing on Mr. MacAllister's case had taken all day and had been hard fought, but Chalmers had succeeded in persuading the judge that, of all the many reasons the magistrates had given for refusing to enrol Mr. MacAllister as a voter, only one had any potential merit. The judge had agreed that little evidence would be required to settle the matter and had ordered a further hearing just a few weeks hence to hear the case in full. It was a significant victory. Cases often ran for years in the Court of Session, and Chalmers had advised Mr. MacAllister that the magistrates were likely to try to push the case beyond the coming election to deprive it of any practical purpose. That they had failed to do so was down to a number of factors: David's meticulously prepared submissions, Chalmers' calm, confident delivery and finally the judge's goodwill. For of course, the judge knew and liked Chalmers well. It was part of what the client paid for when he chose to instruct the man.

After the hearing, Mr. MacAllister insisted on buying them all a dram to celebrate. It turned into considerably more than a few drams, and now David found himself weaving his way home, feeling thoroughly intoxicated after far too much whisky and no dinner.

He had entirely forgotten that it was Tuesday and that Euan was due to come to his rooms. He only remembered when he got to his front door and found the lad slumped outside, dozing.

"Dear God," David exclaimed. "I forgot you were coming! Come in and get warm. I'll get a fire going. It's damn near freezing tonight."

Once he'd unlocked the door, David pulled the younger man to his feet and guided him inside, aware of his own unsteady gait.

"Sorry, Davy," Euan muttered as he allowed David to steer him into the sitting room. "I never meant to fall asleep. I just thought I'd sit and wait awhile."

"Don't be daft," David replied, mortified. He gently pushed Euan towards an armchair and turned away to light a candle. "My fault entirely. I've been preoccupied—but that's no excuse."

Once the candle was glowing, he bent to light the fire that Ellen, the maidservant, had already made up and put a kettle on before heading to the larder to find out what he had to eat. He felt suddenly ravenously hungry.

Ellen had fetched him some cold meat pie for his dinner and left it in the larder with a pot of plums. He got out two plates and divided the pie roughly between them, adding a hunk of cheese, a scattering of oatcakes and a couple of the plums to each plate to bulk out the simple meal.

When he got back to the sitting room, the fire was blazing and Euan was looking more awake, chafing his hands in front of the flames. He smiled wanly over his shoulder at David, then frowned.

"You don't need to feed me again, Davy."

David made an impatient sound. "Doesn't it occur to you I

might be hungry myself? It's customary to offer some of what you're eating to any guest you have, didn't you know?"

Euan flushed and accepted the plate that David thrust none too politely at him.

David fetched cutlery from the sideboard drawer and passed it over silently, nodding at Euan's muttered thanks before he settled himself on the other armchair, and they began to eat.

David ate his pie quickly, almost groaning with pleasure over the short, lardy pastry and cold, pressed ham. He made short work of the cheese and oatcakes too, then set his plate aside and leaned back in his chair with a plum.

The immediate, sharp sourness of the purple skin drew a rush of saliva into his mouth. The mellow sweetness of the golden flesh that followed was like nectar. He ate the fruit in a few bites, dropping the stone onto his plate, then rose to lift the now-boiling kettle from the fire.

"I'll just get us a toddy," he said, giving Euan an overly wide berth as he walked past him with the heavy kettle. Experienced with intoxication, David was a careful drunk, compensating expertly for his lack of coordination with slow, practised movements and over-precise diction.

In the kitchen, he mixed up some of the hot water with whisky and honey, pouring the mix into two pewter cups and stirring them thoroughly to melt the honey.

"What's in this?" Euan asked, frowning, when David handed one of the cups to him. "I don't drink spirits." He looked every the inch the theology student then, with his thin, earnest face, and his slender, scholarly fingers wrapped round the pewter cup.

"There's a bit of whisky in it, but the hot water burns off the spirit," David replied. "It'll stop you catching a chill from sleeping on my stoop."

Euan took a swallow and immediately coughed. "How much whisky did you put in?"

"A good measure," David admitted with a chuckle. "It'll warm you up,"

Euan looked unconvinced but lifted the cup and gingerly sipped at it. "It's not your first dram tonight, is it?"

"No," David said, relaxing his head against the back of his chair. "I've already had a few."

"Yes, I can tell."

David raised a self-mocking eyebrow. "And I thought I was hiding it so well too."

"You are, actually. The most telling thing is how much more relaxed you seem." Euan paused. "And you smile more. Is this who you really are, Davy?"

David chuckled again. "*In vino veritas*? No, it's just that all drunks smile. When they're drunk anyway."

"Are you a drunk, then?"

David sighed. "At times."

"Peter used to say that drunkenness is what keeps the working man down. He gave up spirits when he was my age, and he never let me drink at all." The lad lifted his cup and drained the rest of the contents. His eyes were watering when he lowered the cup—there was still a good bite of spirit in there, despite the hot water. "Can I have another?"

David stared at him for a long moment, then shook his head. "You should listen to your brother."

"Ah, but I can't now, can I? Not ever again."

David caught a glimpse of Euan's thin face, etched with an expression of unbearable grief, before he turned his head away to hide.

It was a forceful reminder of why the lad was here.

"Listen—I have some news for you," David said impulsively. He'd been swithering over whether to share his suspicions about Balfour with the lad, but suddenly it seemed wrong to hold them back.

Euan's head came up at that. "News?"

David proceeded to tell Euan about his unexpected

meeting with Balfour at Chalmers's house and the mention of Bella Galbraith at the dinner table. He didn't tell Euan that he'd met Balfour before that night, nor did he mention their argument on the way home. He concentrated instead on the facts that Bella Galbraith's father had once been an advocate, that Balfour knew her, and that Balfour himself was a tall, dark, anglicised Scot.

"It must be him," Euan said excitedly when David was finished. "This man is Lees."

"Not necessarily," David said carefully. "There are many men like Balfour in Edinburgh. Rich Scots who come home infrequently. And he certainly didn't seem to be harbouring a passion for the girl—just mentioned he was going to call on her."

"Well, of course he wouldn't speak of his feelings at a dinner with strangers! He only told Peter about the girl because he was drunk. I'm sure it must be him, but even if not, Isabella is certainly real, and she will lead me to him!" The lad was vibrating with excitement, the grief all chased away now. "When will I be able to see him, do you suppose? I met Lees a couple of times. I'm positive I'd know him again."

Something in David cavilled at Euan's wish to see Balfour, even though he knew it was ridiculous to object when David was the one who'd raised the possibility that Lees and Balfour were one and the same. He felt suddenly sober.

"Chalmers's daughter mentioned an assembly she's going to this Saturday with Bella Galbraith," he said slowly. "Lees might be there, I suppose—whoever he is."

Euan was now flushed with excitement. "Could we go to this assembly?"

David paused, considering. "It may be a public assembly I can purchase tickets for. I'm not sure, but I can find out easily enough. You'll need to wear some of my clothes, though, and behave like a gentleman."

Euan nodded eagerly. "Whatever it takes. I'll be guided by

you." He paused, then added earnestly, "And I will repay you for the tickets. It will take some time, but I swear you will not be out of pocket."

David shook his head. "It doesn't matter, it'll be a few shillings at most." When Euan opened his mouth to protest, David continued determinedly. "But I do need something from you."

"Anything."

"I need you to agree to be cautious. I know you are eager to confront Lees, but you must understand that—whoever he may be—he will not be like you. His business is violence and deceit. You cannot assume that he will act honourably—"

"You don't need to worry," Euan replied, frowning. "I'm not the innocent you seem to think I am."

"When I was your age—"

"All of four years ago?" Euan laughed and shook his head. "Look, Davy, I'm not from a wee farm village like you. I grew up in a rough town. You had to be tough to get by there. And I was. I *am*."

David sighed. "Just be careful. Promise me you won't do anything rash without telling me."

"So long as I tell you first, I can be rash, then?" Euan chuckled, suppressing his smile when he saw David's frown. "All right. I promise."

After a brief silence, David asked, "Where are you sleeping just now?"

Euan looked away, seeming embarrassed. "I have a place," he said. "It's just a share of a room, a place to bed down at night, but it does me all right."

"Where is it?"

"Not far from here—just at the other end of the Cowgate."

David could imagine what it would be like. A tiny room in a filthy close housing ten times as many people as it was fit for, most of them likely drunk, poor beggars.

"You could stay here if you like. I've plenty of—"

"No." Euan's tone was implacable, his expression all offended pride.

"Fair enough. But the offer stands, if you ever need it."

Euan insisted on going soon after that, promising to return in a day or two. He slipped out David's front door and went down the dark stairwell, as insubstantial as a shadow, and as quiet.

David thought of Euan making his way down the steep hill to the Cowgate where it lurked at the bottom of Blair Street. David had started his life in Edinburgh down there, as a student. All life was there, from skilled workers trapped there by the capital's high rents, to manual labourers and students eking out a living, to the poor and the destitute living in loathsome poverty, stuck away in half rooms and hidey holes.

Euan was walking down the hill of Blair Street right now, down into darkness and filth and rows of rickety tenements that looked like bent old women. What a world away from the New Town, with its grand townhouses and symmetrical architecture. What a world away from all that privilege and power.

David straddled those worlds now. Poised at the top of Blair Street, perched on the edge of the Old Town's squalor, ready to fly. Desperate to fly. Even as guilt made him look over his shoulder and wonder what he'd lose when he flew, and if he'd ever regret its loss or just be glad to have left it all behind him.

CHAPTER NINE

"Do you think he'll be there tonight?" Euan asked while David tied one of his own cravats about the lad's neck. In the four days since David had last seen him, Euan seemed to have become even more convinced that Balfour must be Lees.

"I don't know," David said patiently, adding, "I hope you're remembering your promise."

"Of course," Euan replied. "I won't do anything rash—not without speaking to you first."

"That's good. And you'll need to keep an open mind too. Murdo Balfour and Lees aren't necessarily the same man."

"That too," Euan said, though he seemed distracted.

"Remember, the key is Isabella Galbraith." David stepped back to eye Euan's appearance with a critical eye. "We might be able to gauge something from her reaction to Balfour."

"Or his reaction to her."

David shrugged. "Yes, but be alert to other men around her. Don't only look at Balfour."

"I won't—if I get in."

"You'll be fine. It's a public assembly, we have tickets, and you look very respectable. Don't tug at your cravat."

Euan dropped his hand. "It feels tight," he complained. "And these shirt points keep poking my chin."

David smiled. "If you were a fashionable young gent, you'd think those shirt points far too low. You should see how high some wear them."

Euan snorted disdainfully. "Well, I'm no' one of that lot," he exclaimed, his cultivated accent slipping with his scorn.

"Tonight you are," David said firmly. "Tonight you're James Grant, a minister's son studying in Glasgow and visiting me."

"I know, I know. But I feel like an idiot," Euan muttered.

David clapped him on the shoulder. "You look fine." He looked better than fine, actually. In the tailored clothes of a bookish young gentleman from a decent family, he looked carelessly handsome, if a bit thin, his good looks more obvious now that he was clean and well dressed.

"Come on," David said, settling his hat on his head. "George Street's a bit of a walk."

Thankfully it was a dry night, though cold. They walked briskly, arriving at the Assembly Rooms to find themselves in a crowd of patrons awaiting entry. Young ladies in pastel gowns fluttered around, chattering like a flock of birds while watchful mothers and put-upon fathers looked on. The gentlemen arrived in twos and threes, greeting each other heartily while surreptitiously watching the ladies.

There was no one David knew among the waiting patrons. He and Euan stood side by side, silent amongst the merriment as the crowd moved slowly forward.

Eventually they gained entry to the ballroom. It was a huge room, second only, David had heard, to the Great Room in Bath. It was amazingly bright too, glowing with the flickering light of what looked like hundreds of candles. Candlelight made everything look so much better than it really was, David thought. It softened all the harsh angles of daytime things, hiding imperfections and flattering the plainest faces.

"Come on," David said, tugging Euan's arm. "Let's get something to drink."

He paid a few coins for two cups of punch—weak, cloudy stuff—while Euan stood stiffly beside him. They sipped it as they watched the entrance to the ballroom for new arrivals.

Would Balfour turn up? Surely he would. He had intimated as much to Elizabeth Chalmers over dinner after all. But perhaps he was just being polite? Perhaps even now he was in bed with some pretty, willing boy? That thought made David feel oddly hollow, and he found himself wondering how it might have been if he'd accepted Balfour's invitation the other night. If he'd walked up those stairs with him and gone into his house, into his bedchamber. Stripped for him and dropped to his knees again.

Realising he was growing hard, David thrust his thoughts away and drained his cup of punch, wishing it was whisky. He returned his attention determinedly to the entrance.

It was almost a full hour before they saw anyone David knew, and it wasn't Balfour. It was Elizabeth Chalmers with her mother and next oldest sister, whose name David had already forgotten.

When Elizabeth spied David, her ordinary face lit up with a bright smile, and she raised a gloved hand at him in a tiny wave. Mrs. Chalmers noticed Elizabeth's distraction, and her gaze followed her daughter's, a frown drawing her eyebrows together when she saw that David was the object of the younger woman's attention.

He bowed at the three ladies, eliciting bobbing curtseys from Elizabeth and her sister and a cold nod from their mother before she brusquely moved the girls along without detouring to allow them to speak to David. Elizabeth sent him a regretful glance as she trailed her mother.

"Who's that girl?" Euan asked, staring after them with an arrested expression.

"Which one?"

"The one who smiled at you. With the sparkling eyes."

David smothered a smile, amused that even single-minded Euan could be distracted by a pair of sparkling eyes. "She's the girl who's friends with Isabella Galbraith—Elizabeth Chalmers. The other girl is her sister, and the older woman is their mother."

Euan considered for a moment. "We'd better keep an eye on them, then."

"We'll do better than that," David replied. "We'll ask them to dance. This is an assembly, you know."

Euan looked horrified, hunted. "I don't know how to dance," he said under his breath.

"Surely you know some country dances?"

"I know lots of them but not any of the ones that are being done here! None of this looks like dancing I've seen. Don't these people know how to enjoy themselves?"

David smiled. He knew what Euan meant. This was nothing like the village dances he'd attended in Midlauder when he was a boy. They'd been both tamer and wilder. No question of an unmarried young man directly asking a single girl to dance with him, though it might be arranged with her parents' agreement. But when the women danced without the men, they lifted their skirts to their knees and laughed and sang, and when the men danced without the women, there was yelling and whooping and such a carry on. More sport than grace in it. David smiled to remember those days. William had loved showing off at such affairs, undertaking absurd feats, like the time he balanced on top of a pyramid of men, swaying at the top so much it made David's gut clench with fear, even as he laughed. He used to grin at David as they danced with the other men, white teeth flashing, all cocky and handsome. William's father would've been mortified if he'd known his son was fraternising with the tenants and labourers. And worse.

This assembly was very different from those long-ago

Midlauder dances. The small twelve-piece orchestra was well dressed and played the music at a stately pace. The dancing was elegantly restrained. And yet the purpose of the evening —to snare a marital prospect—was, if anything, more obvious. Almost offensively so. Something businesslike about the way the dances were transacted, the young ladies' time doled out in small measures. As though they were goods in a grocer's shop to be sampled. Two ounces here and four ounces there.

David's attention began to drift, his gaze traversing the crowd for what felt like the hundredth time, when his attention snagged on a dark, familiar head.

Balfour was half turned from him, deep in conversation with an older lady. His profile was strong, unmistakable. The straight blade of his nose and that firm, determined jaw. The sweep of black hair across his brow. When he smiled at his companion, it seemed to David that the room brightened, as though a sudden breeze had caused the candles to all glow just a little bit more. Balfour's evening clothes seemed twice as elegant as anyone else's in some unidentifiable way. He seemed more assured, more powerful. Taller, broader, more arresting. Even his smile was more engaging. He was simply…more.

Just as David came to that conclusion, Balfour turned his head, and their gazes met.

For an instant, Balfour's expression showed genuine surprise—dark brows elevating, eyes widening—and David felt a surge of satisfaction to have caused that small reaction. But just as quickly, Balfour had himself under control, regaining his customary expression of lazy amusement and raising his cup of punch in a mocking toast.

"Jesus Christ!"

Euan's soft exhalation in David's ear distracted his attention. He turned to the younger man, who was staring across the ballroom at Balfour. Balfour himself had turned back to his own companion. Had he seen Euan? Recognised him?

"Is it him?" David asked, his mouth suddenly dry, a gnawing fear growing in his belly. In his absorption, he had almost forgotten why they were here.

"Yes, I—I think—God, I don't *know*." Euan frowned, uncertain. "If it's not him, it looks damned like him. I need to get a closer look."

David felt suddenly shaky, and his heart was racing. He realised with some dismay that he'd desperately wanted Euan to say no, Balfour wasn't Lees. How absurd. Why should he care one way or the other?

"Did he see you?" he asked Euan calmly, somehow managing to disguise his reaction. "Recognise you?"

"He didn't seem to, but then he was looking at you," Euan replied distractedly, his gaze still on the back of Balfour's head. "I don't think he even glanced my way."

"If he'd known you, surely he'd have shown some reaction? You're standing right beside me, after all."

Euan sent him a curious look, as if wondering why David was being so vehement.

"Why don't you try to get closer to him," David added. "It might be easier to tell. I'll go and look for the Chalmers girls and see if I can find out if Isabella Galbraith has turned up yet."

Euan nodded. "All right," he said, but he didn't move immediately, and a muscle in his cheek shifted.

"Are you?" David asked, frowning. "All right, I mean?"

"Yes, it's just I've never been at something like this before. What if someone—" Euan broke off, as though unsure what the worst thing was that could happen, and looked helplessly at David.

"You'll be fine," David assured him. "You have a ticket. You've every right to be here. Just circulate and try to get a look at Balfour. I'll see you back here, at this pillar, at nine o'clock."

Euan nodded again and this time he moved away, towards Balfour, while David turned on his heel in pursuit of the Chalmers ladies.

After a few minutes of strolling round the ballroom, David found Elizabeth, sitting with a group that included her mother and sister. Forcing aside his usual shyness, David approached, addressing his first remarks to her mother.

"Mrs. Chalmers, how pleasant to see you. I trust you are having a good evening?"

She eyed him coolly but didn't cut him, thankfully. "I am, Mr. Lauriston. And you?"

"Yes, thank you."

"I see your companion is not with you?"

"He was waylaid by an acquaintance," David fibbed. "So I took the opportunity to come over. I was hoping that one of your lovely daughters might deign to dance with me." He glanced at the Misses Chalmers and smiled. Elizabeth pinkened. The other one looked amused.

Mrs. Chalmers gestured at her daughters with one satin-gloved hand, as if to say, *Well, ask them, then, if you must,* and turned back to the older lady she had been speaking with before David's arrival.

"Would you care to dance, Miss Elizabeth?"

"How kind," Elizabeth replied, her cheeks scarlet as she consulted her dance card. "I am free for the next set, if that would suit?"

"Excellent. And—" He turned to the other sister whose name he couldn't remember, pausing for too long before glancing at Elizabeth again. She seemed to realise his difficulty.

"Catherine, do let me see your dance card," she interjected. "Oh, look, you have the one after next free. That would be perfect as we're both dancing the set after." She looked up at David again, eyes twinkling, and said, "Would that suit, Mr. Lauriston?"

He smiled, amused, and said, "Oh, that would suit me very well, Miss Chalmers," before realising he was really addressing the wrong sister, and turned his attention back to Catherine who was watching him with apparent interest. "If it suits, Miss Catherine, of course," he added humbly.

Catherine gave him a dry look and assured him it suited her well enough.

He made small talk with the two young ladies for a few more minutes before the next set began, a rather dull country dance that David knew sufficiently to perform confidently. He offered his arm to Elizabeth to lead her onto the floor, and she laid a white-gloved hand on his dark sleeve. She was a small woman, and her fussy blue gown drowned her a little. It had ruffles everywhere: little ones round the neckline and sleeves and three deep ones at the hem. The skirt of the gown seemed to be hampering her as she walked. David had to slow his usual pace to accommodate her. It made her seem fragile to him, and, for a moment, he was almost attracted to her. Not sexually, but to the feeling of protecting someone smaller and weaker than himself.

They joined an incomplete set, smiling at their neighbours and introducing themselves while they waited for the music to start. At last the orchestra began.

"You look very nice this evening, Mr. Lauriston," Elizabeth said breathlessly on their first pass.

He smiled back. "As do you, Miss Chalmers. That shade of blue looks very well on you."

That much was true, and David liked the way her eyes sparkled a little at the compliment. She had such a very responsive face. He was never in any doubt as to what she thought. There was something rather intoxicating about making another person so obviously, and easily, happy.

"...your Miss Chalmers is enamoured with you..."

"You are very kind," she said softly, and the expression on her face was tender and exposed.

"*...because you're beautiful, virtuous and utterly unthreatening...*"

David swallowed. All the pleasure he felt in paying Elizabeth a compliment fled. Was he encouraging something he ought not to encourage? Might she interpret his kindness wrongly? And would it be cruel to allow that? He felt suddenly unsure and was glad when the dance parted them.

By the time they came together again, David had himself back under control. He asked after her younger sisters.

"Maria and Jane have been to private dances before, but Mother decided they were too young to come to a public assembly," Elizabeth said, smiling mischievously. "They are wild with envy over Catherine and I being allowed to come, so although I shall officially remark that they are very well, in truth, they are gnashing their teeth at home with Father."

David chuckled. "Judging by how much time they spent talking about a much less grand-sounding assembly at dinner a few nights ago, I should imagine that they are quite devastated."

"Oh, quite," Elizabeth agreed merrily, and he thought how very almost-pretty she looked when she was amused and how much he simply liked her. It occurred to him then that he *could* actually imagine being married to her. He would never desire her, but he would be fond of her and respect her, and she could give him so much. A place in the world, a family, a home. The only thing there would never be between them was passion.

And would that even matter? Would he miss that?

Would she? She was a gently reared girl after all. She wouldn't expect passion in her marriage, would she?

For a few moments, the strangely appealing thought took hold. Perhaps Balfour was not as wrong as David had first supposed when he suggested that David could marry this girl. Perhaps he was capable of the sort of compromise that marriage would entail.

Was he? Capable of setting aside his unnatural desires forever?

His heart sank. He knew he wouldn't be able to do it. He wouldn't want to lapse, but he would do so. He only had to remember the way he'd felt when he'd seen Balfour across the room earlier this evening; how it had felt, suddenly, as though there was no one else in the room. How desire, hot and swift, had risen in him. Those feelings were very different from the tepid protectiveness he felt for this girl. Those feelings were deeply compelling, demanding, all-consuming.

"Mr. Lauriston?" Elizabeth was looking at him with raised brows, and he realised, embarrassed, that the dance had come to an end. He bowed hurriedly and Elizabeth curtseyed; then she set her hand on his arm, and he took her back to her seat.

Two more ladies had joined the group by the time they got back, an older, handsome woman who was deep in conversation with Mrs. Chalmers, and a beautiful girl of around twenty with black hair and skin as pale as new-fallen snow. She was several inches taller than the other ladies in the group, and her striking amber-coloured eyes were level with David's own when Elizabeth introduced them.

"This is my very particular friend, Miss Isabella Galbraith," she said. "We went to the same ladies' seminary and have been friends for a few years now, haven't we, Bella?"

Isabella smiled remotely. "Yes, the very best of friends."

"And this is Mr. Lauriston," Elizabeth continued. "He's an advocate, Bella. He's working on a case with Father just now."

"I'm pleased to make your acquaintance, Miss Galbraith," David said, bowing over the lady's proffered hand. "Perhaps you would do me the honour of dancing with me later?"

"Of course," she replied coolly. She consulted her empty

dance card and, after an almost insulting pause, suggested a set to which David politely agreed. Once that was taken care of, she turned away to speak with her mother again. Elizabeth frowned at her friend's back, plainly disgruntled on David's behalf. When she glanced at David again, it was with an apologetic expression, and he could see she was caught in a quandary. If she made excuses for Miss Galbraith, she was acknowledging that the other girl had indeed been rude. And since David had maintained a blank expression throughout their exchange, Elizabeth wasn't certain he'd noticed. She wasn't to know that David cared little what Isabella Galbraith thought of him. He only wanted a chance to talk with her to see what, if anything, he could discover from her.

The starting up of the orchestra for the next set saved them both from an awkward exchange. David excused himself and made his way over to where Catherine Chalmers sat to claim her for the next set. She stood up quickly, apparently pleased to get away from the two matrons she was sitting between.

It was a more complicated dance this time, and it took all of David's concentration just to get the steps vaguely right. Catherine kept him mostly correct with sharp nudges to his side, tugs of his sleeve and hissed instructions. By the time the dance was over, David was sure he must have more than a few bruises.

He led Catherine back to the group of ladies to discover that Balfour was there, speaking with Isabella Galbraith, Mrs. Galbraith and Elizabeth. Balfour's gaze sought David's as David led Catherine towards them.

"Good evening, Mr. Lauriston," he said. "Are you enjoying the dancing?"

David smiled politely, consciously disguising the jittery excitement that danced in his gut at this, his second sight of Balfour this evening. He was good at hiding his nerves. The first few minutes of any court hearing were always torture for him, but he'd learned to take deep, calming breaths without inflating his chest or obviously taking in air. He'd learned to bear silences—silences were necessary if you were to get hold of yourself so that your voice, when it emerged, was calm and clear and certain.

"I am not much of a dancer, my lord," he replied. "But the ladies have taken pity on me."

There was a duet of protests at this from Elizabeth and Catherine.

"It seems the ladies disagree," Balfour pointed out with a smile.

"They are very kind."

"Did you come alone this evening?" Balfour asked then. His expression held nothing beyond mild curiosity, but David couldn't help thinking the question was significant, and that Balfour meant him to realise that. That he knew already that David had come with someone. Possibly even why that person was here.

"I came with a friend."

"A friend?"

It was an invitation to disclose more, but David had no intention of saying anything beyond that which was entirely necessary.

"Yes—and I should go and find him, actually. Please do excuse me." Without waiting for a response, he bowed to the ladies, including them all in the polite gesture, then turned around and walked in the opposite direction, his heart pounding. Immediately, he felt foolish. He should have stayed longer, observed Balfour with Miss Galbraith, tried to get a sense of how well they knew each other. He'd allowed his own nerves to chase him away and wasted an opportunity in the process.

It was already past nine o'clock, and he had to walk round the ballroom twice before he found Euan, skulking on the fringes of a large, merry group, none of whom appeared to notice he wasn't with them.

"Where have you been?" Euan muttered, peeling away from the group when David approached. "I waited at the pillar for ten minutes. I thought you'd gone."

"I told you I was going to dance. I danced a set with each of the Chalmers girls, so that took a bit of time. And I've got to go back and dance with Miss Galbraith soon. Did you get any closer to Lord Murdo?"

"Aye."

"And?"

Euan paused. "It's not him."

Relief flooded David, making his legs feel suddenly weak and trembly. He wanted to find a chair and sink into it, put his head between his knees and just breathe for a moment. The strength of his own reaction stunned him speechless. He tried to use the same skills he'd just employed in conversation with Balfour to hide that reaction from Euan, but he couldn't prevent himself visibly swallowing and felt sure Euan must notice.

"Are you certain?" he said at last.

"I think so."

David glanced sharply at Euan, frowning as he took in Euan's troubled expression. "You *think* so?"

Euan shook his head unhappily. "He looks like him! But no." He said the last word with what sounded like reluctance. "No, I'm sure it's not him."

"Then what? Do you think he's related to Lees? Is the resemblance a family one?"

Euan nodded. "It must be. It's uncanny, Davy."

So it seemed Balfour was involved with Lees in some way, then, even if only as a kinsman. That knowledge made David wonder why Balfour was really in Scotland, why he'd been in Stirling on the very day of Baird and Hardie's execution. Coincidence?

Or was he here because he took orders from the same masters as his kinsman?

That last thought made David feel as though he was falling, his gut spasming in sudden alarm. David had revealed his sympathies for the weavers' cause to Balfour without much thought at all. Until this moment, when he was faced with the reality that Balfour *had* to be connected to it all, he hadn't considered how imprudent it was to be so frank. Now his unwise words, spoken into the anonymity of night as he walked at Balfour's side, seemed arrogantly naïve, and he burned with regret.

He gave a sigh, forcing those unhelpful thoughts aside. There was nothing to be done about his foolishness.

"What now?" he asked.

"You dance with the Galbraith lass? See what you can find out from her?" Euan suggested.

"All right. You could come and meet her too, if you like," David said.

Euan paused for a long moment, then shook his head. "I don't want her to see me. I'm thinking that I could follow her after the assembly—watch her house for a bit. If Lees is that keen on her, hopefully he'll turn up there at some point. It's my best chance of finding him. He's not going to turn up here tonight, not now."

David nodded. "Agreed. All right, I'll go back now. My set with Miss Galbraith is the one after this one. I'll see what I can find out from her before we go."

Isabella Galbraith was ten times more beautiful than her friend Elizabeth, and just as many times colder. When David arrived to claim her for their set, she stated baldly that she had a headache coming on and didn't feel terribly like dancing. Undaunted by her rudeness—though Elizabeth looked mortified on his behalf—David proposed a stroll around the ballroom instead, suggesting it might help clear her head.

Miss Galbraith couldn't say no to that without being even more obviously rude. She stood reluctantly, placed her hand on the arm David offered, and they began to slowly perambulate the room.

For a few minutes, David kept the conversation light and general. Miss Galbraith was coolly polite and almost monosyllabic in her responses. Eventually, he decided to take a more direct tack.

"Have you spent much time in London, Miss Galbraith? Your father is a politician, is he not?"

"I've spent some time there," she replied. "But I prefer Edinburgh."

"Oh? And why is that?"

She was very lovely, but her smile was like a little bit of winter. "The young ladies of London are chiefly concerned with fashion and entertainment, I find."

It was the first chink he'd seen in her formidable armour. A slight, distant smile graced her pretty lips, and her gaze was aloof. She was proud, this one. Confident of her superiority to everyone around her.

"Perhaps that is the sort of lady London gentlemen prefer?" David offered.

"Not all of them," she answered too quickly to have given the question any real thought.

"No?" He was used to reading people in court. And he sensed in Isabella Galbraith a desire to confide, to boast, one that possibly warred with a need to be discreet. It was perhaps no bad thing that she considered him so below her notice.

"Some gentlemen like ladies who are well educated and who have opinions of their own," she said, and there was a hint of reproof in her voice, as though she thought he must reside in the other camp.

"Having had the privilege of conversing with Miss Chalmers on several occasions," David said truthfully, "I have certainly found her opinions most stimulating. You and Miss Chalmers were educated together, were you not?"

"We were." Miss Galbraith's smile was minutely warmer now. "At Miss Stair's Seminary."

David steered Miss Galbraith round a group of gentlemen who noted her beauty with covert glances though their conversation continued without pause. Once past them, David pressed home his advantage.

"So, do I take it that you have met at least *one* gentleman in London who is stimulated not only by beauty but also by intelligence?"

She actually blushed at that question, her eyelids lowering briefly to mask her gaze from him. Her proud expression seemed to soften a little.

"Perhaps," she said, then added breezily, "They are not all dandies and rakes, at any rate."

"No," David dared. "Take Lord Murdo, for example."

She glanced at him sharply, and he maintained his bland look with difficulty.

"I'm not sure what you seek to make Lord Murdo an example of, Mr. Lauriston," she said. "Perhaps you could explain."

"I just meant he seems an intelligent fellow," David replied carefully, aware he'd somehow put her on her guard.

"Well, I can't argue with that," Miss Galbraith replied tartly. Her manner suggested she knew him well and that there was little love lost between them. On her side at least.

"Have you known him long?" David dared, adding, "He mentioned he knew you when I dined with the Chalmers earlier this week."

"Oh, I've known Lord Murdo for years. He's older than me, but our families are well acquainted. His aunt and my mother are particular friends." She paused, then added, "I've seen him more often lately. It seems that everywhere I turn, there he is!" She gave a nervous laugh then, and it was perhaps the most betraying thing of all in their conversation.

He realised that she didn't like Balfour one little bit.

———

David didn't get any more out of Miss Galbraith. They finished their perambulation of the ballroom, and he delivered her back to her mother, who was in conversation with Balfour and Elizabeth Chalmers. They stopped talking as David and Miss Galbraith drew closer, and Balfour glanced at David, raising a brow. "Dancing again, Lauriston?"

David smiled politely. "Miss Galbraith did not care to dance. We took a stroll about the ballroom instead."

"You don't care to dance, Bella?" Balfour said. "What nonsense is this?"

"I wish you wouldn't call me Bella," she said curtly.

"Isabella." Her mother said her name so blandly that it could almost not have been a reproof, but Miss Galbraith flushed.

Balfour frowned. "I've called you Bella since we were children."

David saw her making an effort to be calm and ladylike. "Well, I'm not a child anymore," she said quietly. "Isabella will do very well."

"Very well. Have it your way. Isabella it shall be—in public." He flicked a speck of lint from his immaculate black evening coat. "But you can't stop me thinking of you as Bella."

She scowled, and her mother laughed. "It's refreshing to see you around my daughter, Lord Murdo. I grow tired of tripping over young men kissing the hem of her gown."

Miss Galbraith's jaw tightened, and Balfour smiled enigmatically. "Oh, it's hardly surprising, ma'am," he said. "Bella

—sorry, Isabella—is so very beautiful. Hem-kissing is practically compulsory in such circumstances."

Mrs. Galbraith laughed again, but her daughter looked irritable, and David felt something close to nausea twist in his guts.

"It's too bad of you to tease her so, my lord," Elizabeth Chalmers said, smiling in that calm way of hers. "I'm not surprised she prefers to be called Isabella. It's a very noble name, I think."

"Quite so," Balfour said, smothering a smile. "And well said, Miss Chalmers."

Two new gentlemen arrived then, to claim both young ladies for the next set. Isabella demurred, pleading the headache again, and her partner withdrew. David heard her mother chiding her as she drew her away to sit down.

"Please excuse me," David said, smiling at Elizabeth and her partner and ignoring Balfour. "I must find my friend again. We have to be on our way soon."

Elizabeth halted as her partner attempted to lead her away, a little pucker between her brows. "Oh, Mr. Lauriston, must you leave so soon?" she exclaimed.

"I'm afraid so. I did say I would leave with my friend."

"Oh, what a shame!"

"The music is starting, Miss Chalmers," her partner said anxiously, and she looked at him as though she'd forgotten he was there. "Oh, I do beg your pardon, Mr. MacNeill! We mustn't miss our dance." She threw one last look at David as her partner led her away. "Good night, Mr. Lauriston. I hope we will see you again soon."

"Good night, Miss Chalmers."

David made to walk away then, but Balfour's voice in his ear, at once soft and oddly threatening, halted him in his tracks.

"Is your friend the fair-headed youth I saw you with earlier?"

David turned to face him. Although there was no smile on the other man's face—no expression at all, in fact—there was a trace of amusement there. This was, David realised, Balfour's basic expression. Anything else the man showed was a layer on top. It made him look as though he was perpetually at one remove from everyone and everything. Always superior, always observing.

"Yes, that's him," David said shortly. "And he's waiting for me, so if you'll excuse—"

"Is he your lover?"

David laughed in surprise. It was so absurd. "What on earth—"

"Is he?" Balfour was still faintly smiling, but the question emerged like a bullet from a musket, setting David back on his heels. He couldn't imagine where this had come from, but he didn't like the focused interest Balfour was showing in Euan MacLennan.

"He's a pretty lad," Balfour went on. "How long have you known him?"

"Awhile," David said shortly. "If you'll excuse me—"

Balfour's hand shot out, gripping David's upper arm.

Astonished, David tugged his arm free. "How dare you!" he hissed. He cast a nervous glance around, wondering if anyone had noticed Balfour's sudden aggression.

"Are you lovers or not?"

David stared at the other man. Was there a hint of strain in the faint smile that played over Balfour's well-shaped mouth? After a moment, David stepped back, putting two feet of clear space between them, and made a brief, watchful bow.

"If you'll excuse me," he said, ignoring Balfour's question, "I really must be going."

And with that, he turned and walked quickly away.

CHAPTER TEN

David found Euan hovering on the edges of the same large group as before, shoulders hunched, lips pinched closed. He wasn't comfortable in these surroundings, among these people. If he still wanted to join the Kirk, he would have to become so at some stage.

"There you are," Euan said, looking relieved as David approached. Under his breath, he added, "Did you find out anything useful?"

"No," David replied shortly, striving to disguise how shaken he felt after that odd exchange with Balfour. "Come on. I'll tell you about it outside."

They collected their coats and hats and emerged into a cold, clear night. A row of carriages stretched down George Street, waiting for their owners to reclaim them. Did one of those carriages belong to Balfour, David wondered? Balfour's house was very close but his very proper evening slippers were quite inappropriate for damp, chilly cobbles. David couldn't imagine Balfour would be going home on foot.

David's footwear might not be as elegant as Balfour's, but it was eminently more suited to walking, and his heavy greatcoat was a welcome guard against the cold. He eyed Euan's thinner version with concern.

"You must be freezing."

"I'm fine," Euan replied with a tight smile. "You must've gone soft if you think this is cold." But David saw him shiver and bury his hands in his pockets.

"I'll bet that room of yours is freezing in this weather," David said, knowing that Euan's "room" was probably no better than a space on a bare floor.

The lad shrugged. "The cold doesn't bother me."

"You're welcome to stay with me," David offered with studied casualness. "I can't offer you a proper bed, but I could make you a reasonably comfortable pallet on the floor. You won't freeze at least."

Euan shook his head. "I want to see where this Galbraith lass lives. I'm going to wait till she comes out and follow her home."

"Tonight? Is that really necessary? You know she lives on Heriot Row. It shouldn't be too difficult to find her tomorrow."

"I'd rather do it now, when it's dark," Euan insisted. "Loitering round that fancy part of town during the day when someone might see me isn't a good idea."

"As opposed to loitering out here now, waiting for people to leave an assembly? Believe me, this looks just as suspicious, if not more."

"I know that." Euan frowned, his brows drawing together. "But I'm not going to hang around out here. I'm going to hide in that close over there. Come on, I'll show you."

He grabbed David's sleeve and towed him across the street, pulling him into a narrow close opposite the Assembly Rooms. Although the darkness swallowed them up quickly, they could still see the well-lit entrance reasonably well from their shadows.

"You see? I'll watch the entrance from here," Euan said softly. "Then follow her home."

"She probably has a carriage waiting," David pointed out.

"I can run. I'm fast too."

David peered at Euan. He couldn't make out much in the shadows, just the languid slouch of his long body against the close wall and the glitter of his eyes as he turned to look at David.

"But—why? Do you really think Lees will turn up at her house? It seems unlikely, don't you think? He didn't come tonight."

A shrug. "He might, and that makes it worthwhile trying. You found the Galbraith girl, even though you didn't expect to."

"And what will you do if he turns up?"

"I'll follow him. Find out his direction."

David paused. "Then what?"

Silence. Euan shifted against the wall, hunching his shoulders more.

"Euan, you promised me that you'd do nothing rash without speaking to me first."

"I know."

"So, if you track down Lees, you'll come and speak to me before you do anything else? Yes?"

After an uneasy pause, Euan spoke, reluctance in his tone. "Davy, if I can, I will, but it may not be easy. If I only get one chance to—"

"No!" David interrupted. "You promised me, Euan. It's all I've asked of you."

Euan levered himself off the wall, shaking his head. He huffed out a sigh. "I shouldn't've promised you that." He sounded resentful. "But I did. So yes, if I find him, I'll tell you first. Will that do?"

"Thank you," David said gravely. "That's all I ask."

"You might as well go home, then." Euan sounded almost sullen. "No sense two of us freezing, especially when you think it's such a waste of time."

David sighed. "I'll wait with you a bit, if you like," he offered. "For company."

Another shrug. "It's up to you."

David took that unenthusiastic response as agreement and pulled his coat more tightly about himself. The night really was cold, with a deep, damp chill in the air that would permeate the marrow of a man's bones if he stood in it long enough.

"What did the Galbraith lassie say when you danced with her?" Euan asked after a while. He was leaning on the wall again, his face turned away, watching the entrance of the Assembly Rooms.

"Not much," David admitted. He outlined their conversation succinctly, describing the girl's reactions to his questions.

"I don't think she likes Lord Murdo," David concluded, "though her mother seems to. She hinted there might be a man in London she favours but didn't mention anyone in particular."

"No one who could be Lees?"

"Not that she mentioned, but I could tell she was being careful."

"It doesn't matter. Lees will turn up at her door eventually," Euan said. "I'm sure of it."

David couldn't help but hope that Euan was wrong, that Lees would stay well away from Isabella Galbraith. He knew how desperately Euan longed to confront the man, but he worried for the lad. For all Euan's insistence that he was tougher than he looked, he wasn't much more than a boy, and his fierce idealism would be no match for a man like Lees.

It would be a long while before Euan would give up waiting for Lees, if the man never appeared. But as determined and committed as Euan was, he would give up eventually. There was nothing in the world like a long, dreary wait for slowly killing every bit of hope in you. David knew that better than anyone.

After Will had left Midlauder, David had waited more than two years for just a glimpse of the friend he'd loved so dearly. But the flame of hope that burned so strongly in David's heart to begin with couldn't keep burning with nothing to fuel it. As letter after letter went unanswered, David's hope had slowly died, till there was nothing but ashes left. And when he'd finally seen Will again, riding through Midlauder on a fine black horse, he hadn't even been surprised when his friend had looked away without speaking. As though they were perfect strangers.

David glanced at Euan. The lad still leaned against the wall in his threadbare coat, staring out the mouth of the close. He looked oddly lost and David was reminded again of himself in his university days, struggling to find a place in a new and very different world. It had been hard, even with the wee bits of money his father had periodically scraped together for him, to get through those years of study. How much harder was it for Euan with his only family torn from him?

As they waited, they talked in a desultory way. David stamped his feet and rubbed his gloved hands together against the cold. Euan didn't seem to feel the cold as badly. He stayed in the same position throughout, leaning against the wall, shoulders hunched and chin burrowed down inside the collar of his coat, but otherwise his lanky frame was still.

"You should go home, Davy," he said eventually. "You're freezing, and it's not as though you can come with me when I follow the lassie anyway."

David *was* freezing. And tired and bored. Nevertheless, he felt a stab of guilt to leave Euan alone here.

"Are you sure? I can stay a bit longer if you want the company."

"To be honest, watching you huff and puff and rub your hands is making me feel the cold more than if I was on my own."

David gave a laugh. "All right, but if you get tired of freezing your arse out here, the offer of a bed stands, no matter the hour."

"Thank you," Euan replied. "But I mean to wait by the girl's door as long as it takes."

"Let me know how you go, at least. You know where I am. Don't leave it too long."

Euan nodded. "I'll call on you. Soon."

David was about to step out of the shadows when Euan's arm shot out, hauling him back. He staggered, his weight landing against the younger man's chest.

"What—?"

"Wait!" Euan hissed. "Look who it is."

A small group had just emerged from the Assembly Rooms—Balfour, Isabella Galbraith and Mrs. Galbraith. Balfour offered an arm to each of the two ladies, and they began to walk down the line of carriages. The carriages and horses soon impaired David's view, but he spotted a groom jumping down from the driver's bench of one of the parked carriages and running round to open a door. That had to be Balfour's carriage.

"They're leaving," Euan said softly. "I'm going to start slowly walking that way now so it won't be obvious I'm following them. Can you wait for a few minutes before you go? We're less likely to be noticed if we come out of here separately."

"Yes, of course," David replied, but he was speaking to the night air. Euan had already sidled out and was gone.

David counted out five full minutes, waiting till Balfour's

carriage began pulling away before he emerged. But as soon as he stepped out, he saw he had made a grave error.

He should have waited a little longer, for on the other side of the road, in the space left by the departing carriage, stood Balfour. He'd put the ladies in the carriage, but he had stayed behind.

Balfour wore a long black evening cloak over his elegant clothes and carried a silver-topped cane. He looked magnificent and untouchable, and he was staring straight at David, standing in the mouth of the close.

David realised, with a dawning sort of awareness, that the expression on his own face probably looked nothing short of horrified. He turned on his heel and started walking quickly away in the opposite direction to that taken by Euan.

What had Balfour thought, seeing David emerge from the shadows of the narrow close, long after he'd left the Assembly Rooms? Given what David had done with Balfour in a similar place less than a month ago, he could make a fair guess, and his face burned at the thought.

He wasn't far from the end of George Street when he heard his name being called. He turned around, unsurprised to see that it was Balfour calling to him—and not walking but actually loping down the street.

Even running down George Street in evening slippers, Balfour somehow managed to look effortlessly masculine. The thought might have made David smile if he hadn't felt so nervous and mortified.

"On your way home, Lauriston?" Balfour said once he'd drawn level with David. The deep voice was as smooth as honey, his breathing unaffected by his exertions.

"Yes."

"Shall we walk together, then?"

"I turn south at the end of the street," David replied flatly. The end of George Street was scarcely fifty yards ahead, not worth the bother of catching up with someone at all.

"Till you turn off, then," Balfour said tightly.

"Fine." David began walking quickly, and Balfour fell into step beside him.

After a moment, Balfour said conversationally, "You never introduced me to your friend, Lauriston. Tell me, was he fucking you in that alleyway?"

David swallowed. He'd been half expecting this, and he kept his answer short, his eyes fixed ahead. "No."

"No? Sucking you, then? Or you him, perhaps? You like that, don't you? On your knees, in the dirt."

David compressed his lips tightly, refusing to answer, and walked more quickly.

"Answer me, damn you!" That demand was accompanied by a hand hauling at his arm, jerking him around bodily to face the other man and witness an expression on Balfour's face he'd not seen before. No trace of humour now.

"It's none of your business," David bit out.

"I beg to differ," Balfour shot back. "You are my business."

"What?"

Suddenly the hand gripping David's arm was pushing, pushing him into a shadowed portico. Taken by surprise, David stepped backwards, his feet tripping a little as Balfour pressed him farther till he was swallowed by shadows and his shoulders hit the wall.

"I've made you my business," Balfour muttered, bracing his hands against the wall on either side of David's head and looking down into David's upturned face.

"Why?" David demanded.

Balfour's eyes glittered. "I wish I knew," he said, and it was such a surprising response that David couldn't think how to reply.

An odd silence bloomed between them, thick with arousal and tension. Balfour pressed closer, till his cock was nudging David's hip. It felt as achingly hard as David's own. David hissed in a shaky breath, all too aware of his heart tripping in his chest and of the heat invading his face. Balfour surrounded David, his breath gusting against David's cheek, his scent invading David's senses. He breached David's carefully constructed walls with his deliberate physical domination, and as much as David resented it, it made him hard and desperate and lustful. It made him want to sink to his knees and take the man in his mouth again.

Lust didn't make you forget all the reasons you shouldn't do something. It just made you not care. It made you not care, even knowing you would regret your actions later. And so it was that when Balfour leaned in a fraction of an inch closer and brushed David's lips with his own, David did nothing to stop him. And when the man shifted his whole body closer, when he took hold of David's face between his gloved hands and slid his sleek tongue into David's mouth in a devouring kiss, David groaned and gripped the edges of Balfour's cloak for dear life.

It was a long, passionate, reckless kiss, and when Balfour at last drew back, David couldn't speak, just stared, shocked, at the other man. Balfour stared back with dark, glittering eyes.

"I played the game wrong with you before," he murmured. "I thought I should appeal to your reason—but I needed to appeal to your body, didn't I? If you think about things too much, you get tied up in knots."

David swallowed. "I'm sure I don't know what you mean."

"I'm doing it again," Balfour said with a rueful smile. "Forget I spoke. Come with me instead."

"Come with you where?"

"To my house. It's just a few minutes' walk away."

"I don't know," David murmured, his gaze shifting away from Balfour. He wanted to go even though he knew he shouldn't. His history was strewn with the wreckage of past regrets.

So what was one more regret? One more sin.

Balfour took David's chin in his fingers and turned his face back, forcing him to meet Balfour's dark gaze. "Don't think so much. Everything gets complicated when you think about it, but this is really very simple. I want you. You want me. And when it's over, we part."

David just looked at Balfour in silence, but something in his expression must have altered, because Balfour smiled.

CHAPTER ELEVEN

By the time they reached Balfour's house, David was having second thoughts. They'd walked here side by side without touching, and the October night had inserted its cold fingers between them, cooling David's lust. He'd had ample time for reflection and the beginnings of regret during the short journey.

And yet, when they reached the townhouse, he didn't hesitate or turn around. He went up the steps to the front door behind Balfour and followed him inside, past the expressionless footman holding the door open and into a house of restrained, masculine elegance.

At Balfour's suggestion, he removed his hat and gloves and greatcoat, handing everything to the footman, who bore his burdens away and brought back a candle to light their way upstairs.

Everything in Balfour's house was rich and elegant, from the long-case mahogany clock in the hall, to the framed paintings they passed as they climbed the stairs, to the long rug that muffled their footsteps as they made their way down the corridor to Balfour's bedchamber.

Balfour swung the door open and stepped aside, inviting David to precede him.

The first thing David noticed was that it wasn't, as he'd expected, a bedchamber. It was a sitting room, with two deep, wing-backed armchairs bracketing either side of a big marble fireplace. The grate glowed with the embers of an earlier blaze and the wasted luxury of a fire burning in an unoccupied room shocked David somewhere in the depths of his Presbyterian soul.

Balfour lit more candles, and now David could see that there was a second room connected to this one. Through an open doorway on the other side of the sitting room, he spied the hulking shape of a large bed, limned by the glow of a second fire. Balfour's bedchamber.

"Would you like some wine?"

Tempted to find a little courage in a glass, David nodded. "Thank you."

Balfour crossed to the sideboard, where a decanter of wine and several glasses waited on a silver tray. The crystal of the decanter sparkled in the candlelight as Balfour lifted it and poured out two glasses of ruby liquid. He strolled over to where David stood in the middle of the room—a slow, cocky stroll—and offered one of the glasses. Their fingertips brushed as David took the glass, and he almost dropped it in his haste to withdraw, fumbling it awkwardly and saving it just in time.

"Careful," Balfour drawled. David flushed. He lifted the glass and took a long swallow to hide his embarrassment. He felt better almost immediately and finished the glass quickly. Only then did he realise that Balfour was leaning against the sideboard watching him, his own glass untouched.

"Another?" Balfour asked with a polite smile.

David had the disturbing feeling the man knew just how much he'd needed that drink. Unsettled, he shook his head and set his glass down, nerves thrumming. The politeness, the hospitality, Balfour's damned *patience*—all of it bothered him. He was used to rough, urgent encounters. Usually in awkward situations. Alleyways and corridors and abandoned places. Never bedchambers. David didn't think that he'd ever been in another man's bedchamber till now.

Scrabbling for familiar ground, he paced towards Balfour, coming to a halt an arm's-breadth away.

"What do you want, then?" he said hoarsely. "I can suck you again, if you'd like."

Balfour put his own wineglass down in an unhurried way and levered himself away from the sideboard. He smiled, to himself it seemed, his lips kicking up at one side, a slight dimple flashing in his cheek.

"Well, since you're asking," he said, finally looking at David, "I'd like to see you naked. And then I'd like to fuck you."

David wished he could control his flushes. He could feel the tidal rush of one spreading upwards from his chest to his throat and farther, till the heat of it scalded his cheeks. "I don't allow anyone to do that."

Balfour smiled. "Do what? See you naked or fuck you?"

"Fuck—penetrate—whatever you want to call it," David replied, face burning.

Balfour stared at him as though he was a fascinating exotic animal. "Why ever not?" A puzzled frown drew his brows together.

Mortified, David made to turn away. "This was not a good idea. I should—"

"Wait."

All evening, it seemed, David had been trying to walk away from Balfour, and all evening, Balfour had been stopping David from leaving. Now he did it again, his hand catching at David's elbow and gently tugging. David turned slowly back.

Balfour's gaze was hot and dark, impossible to look away

from. "I don't have to fuck you—but let me see you without your clothes, hmm?" He smiled and reached for the buttons of David's tailcoat. Embarrassed, David stepped back and raised a hand to rub the back of his neck in an uncomfortable gesture.

Balfour's lips twisted in what looked like reluctant amusement. "All right. I'll go first, but you'll need to help me with this coat. It's a perfect fit and a bugger to get off, if you'll excuse the expression." Without waiting for a reaction, he unfastened the buttons of his own black tailcoat and turned his back on David, opening his arms out as though presenting himself to a valet.

If he wanted to leave, now would be a good time to do so, but David found himself hesitating. The idea of seeing Balfour naked was a powerful lure, one that he was unable to resist.

He stepped forward, sliding his arms over the other man's shoulders to take hold of the lapels of his coat and slowly draw them back, removing the impossibly elegant garment, inch by careful inch. The warmth of Balfour's hard body against his chest and under his hands, his scent—an earthy, spicy smell—it all made David feel heady with an excitement that began to overtake his shame and embarrassment.

Balfour turned round and cast the coat aside. "The rest is easier," he said, lifting his hand to loosen his cravat. And as David stood there, mouth dry and heart pounding, the man stripped his clothes away, his dark, unwavering gaze on David. Waistcoat, cravat and shirt. Breeches, drawers and stockings. Everything, till he was quite naked.

David had wondered what Balfour would look like, under the clothes. If he'd be hairy or smooth. If he'd be as hard and well-honed as David imagined, or if he'd carry a little fat beneath his severely cut clothes.

As Balfour was gradually revealed, David's heart pounded and his breath came faster. His eyes roamed hungrily over the man's big, powerful frame and long, lean muscles—there was not a bit of fat on him. He discovered too that Balfour had a light dusting of hair across his chest, and that the trail of hair narrowed as it travelled down his belly before flaring again around his long, thick cock. The man looked like a warrior, powerful and proud. He seemed unembarrassed by his nudity, and no wonder. Being naked didn't put him at the slightest disadvantage. He still towered over David, still stood before him with the confidence of a general about to command an army. It made David wonder what Balfour would think of David's body when he saw it. Of his slight, wiry frame.

The pained reticence David felt at the thought of revealing himself was a sharp contrast to how he felt looking at Balfour. He itched with the desire to touch the other man, to explore him and discover the scents and textures of his skin, even as he forced himself to keep his hands by his sides. The thought of asking Balfour if he could touch him... Well, he couldn't.

"You now," Balfour said, reaching for him. "Come. I'll help you."

No one had undressed David since he was a child. It felt strange to have another's hands unfastening the buttons of his coat. Strange and exciting.

His coat wasn't so difficult to remove as Balfour's, not having been tailored to a skintight fit against his body. It slid easily from his arms and dropped to the floor while Balfour reached for more intimate articles.

Balfour did it all, all the unbuttoning, untying and drawing away of the layers of David's clothing. David shivered at the hot eagerness in the other man's eyes and the light, brushing touch of his hands as he slowly worked. The man's unashamed passion for his task was unsettling, but it heated David too, a strange mingling of lust and shame.

At last, David was as naked as Balfour himself. He stood before Balfour, feeling deeply vulnerable. The only man he'd ever been fully naked in front of before was William, and that had been entirely innocent. Naked swimming in the burn in Midlauder, when they were little more than boys with narrow, hairless chests.

This was very different.

Balfour seemed gratifyingly pleased with what he saw. His eyes moved over David with restless admiration. He lifted a hand and stroked David's hair. "Such an unusual colour."

"Red hair isn't so uncommon," David murmured.

"It's not the ordinary sort of red hair. It's dark, like old copper. Is that why you don't have freckles? And your skin is like marble." He curved his palms around the apples of David's shoulders, pulling him close enough for their bodies to touch, at last. It was such a relief that David couldn't suppress a soft moan, and Balfour's eyes glittered, enjoying David's reaction.

"I could do this standing up, here and now," he muttered. "But I want to take my time. Come on."

He took David's hand in his own, the clasp of his palm against David's warm and strong, and drew him into the bedchamber, leading him to the bed.

"Lie down," Balfour said, his voice husky. "On your back."

Mouth dry with anticipation, heart pounding with mingled excitement and fear, David did as he was bid. The fire that burned in the grate made the room warm enough that David was able to lie naked atop the bedcovers. The caress of the silken fabric against his naked back was a hedonistic pleasure.

"Spread your legs," Balfour murmured, leaning over David's body to look into his eyes.

"I can't," David whispered, his whole body seizing up, his hands covering his groin automatically.

Balfour smiled slowly. "Yes, you can. Let me make you feel good. Let me suck you."

And God, but the thought of that sinful mouth swallowing him down was all David needed, apparently, to settle his immediate fears. His hands melted away and his legs shifted apart, and soon Balfour was squirming his way down the bed, settling himself between David's thighs.

Was he really going to—

Oh Christ!

The sensation of David's cock being engulfed in Balfour's mouth, almost to the root, made him shout with pleasure. It wasn't that it was an entirely new experience, though he'd more often been the giver than the receiver of this particular pleasure, but it was the first time he'd been taken into a man's mouth with such patient and consummate skill. Balfour didn't just suck him, he worked David's shaft with his tongue and lips, grazed it with his teeth—a snagging, wonderful feeling, that—and he touched David's balls with knowing fingertips, caressing and gently squeezing.

Staring down at Balfour's dark head as the man pleasured him with such care, David felt the oddest bolt of—what was it? Something powerful. Maybe gratitude, though it was bigger than that. He didn't dwell on the thought, though; he simply wasn't able to. The sensations in his cock and balls, the building up of his crisis deep inside him, were far too consuming to permit him to think about anything else.

David had been propped up on his elbows, watching Balfour work, but as the man dipped his head to swallow fully the length of David's cock, David's arms gave out, and he collapsed onto his back with a helpless cry of pleasure. He could come right now, but so long as Balfour was willing to keep doing this, it seemed madness to stop him.

It was then he felt Balfour's fingers graze the crack of his arse. Balfour's mouth was still doing its work, but his hand had definitely moved lower, and David shifted his hips, half rejecting, half encouraging. Just the lightest of touches this, yet the bolt of forbidden pleasure it gave him was intense.

The touching became firmer, and David made a noise of protest deep in his throat, shifting again. Balfour pulled his mouth off David's cock in a long, luscious stroke and looked up at David.

"Don't you like me touching you there?"

"I—I've never allowed anyone—" David broke off, mesmerised by Balfour's playful smile.

"Will you allow me?" Balfour asked softly. "I want to touch you there so very badly. Let me."

Without waiting for an answer, Balfour moved downwards to trail his swollen lips over David's balls.

David cried out at this new sensation, then again when Balfour softly sucked David's sac into his mouth, playing with the delicate contents, using his tongue and lips to tease them.

By now, David was making bargains with himself. So far, and no farther, but he made no protest as Balfour broke past each silent limit until his broad palms were pushing David's thighs even wider and his hot mouth was pressing against the impossibly tender skin below David's scrotum and moving down to probe the tight entrance to his body.

At that first touch of tongue on his anus, David's back arched and his cock bobbed, painting his belly with a dab of fluid. He shouted some profanity, and his hands twisted into the bedcovers. His mind couldn't grasp it—Balfour's mouth —*there!* Soft lips and wet tongue moving against his most intimate flesh. The lewdness of that impossible kiss.

Balfour raised his head from his task, revealing a flush of red across his cheekbones and eyes that were glittering wildly. His gaze travelled over David's exposed body and spread thighs.

"You're beautiful," he said, and, as ridiculous as the words were, David's immediate reaction was to feel moved, though the instant the feeling coalesced into thought, he rejected it. Instead he surrendered himself to the physical sensations that Balfour was igniting in him, ignoring the persistent little voice in his mind that was telling him to stop before this went any further.

Balfour teased David's hole with his mouth while working his shaft with one big hand, and all David could do was pant and moan as he was thoroughly serviced. He'd never experienced anything like this before. Flat on his back in a comfortable bed, being catered to like an emperor.

Just as he was contemplating allowing his crisis to take him, Balfour reared back, and, with his eyes fixed firmly on David's face, inserted his index and middle finger into his own mouth, wetting them thoroughly.

"What…?"

"Don't worry. It's just my fingers. You'll like it, I promise."

And then he was bending down, his mouth engulfing David's cock once more, his fingers circling maddeningly, exploring the entrance to David's body.

Oh God, was he going to allow this? It wasn't buggery, but it would certainly be penetration. Part of another man's body entering his own. Something he'd decided he'd never allow.

Balfour took the decision out of his hands. He pressed his spit-slick finger firmly against David's anus, pushing inwards, making David gasp as his body relented, permitting Balfour entrance. His finger was thick and invasive. Entirely wrong and utterly right. Coupled with the hot, wet silk of Balfour's mouth on his cock, it was the most extraordinary sensation David had felt in all his life.

David felt sure he couldn't possibly last a moment longer. But there was more to come. Balfour rocked his hand, getting David used to the invasion, then withdrew and pressed in again. More this time—two fingers? He couldn't be sure, the hot mouth on his cock a constant distraction. Again the rocking hand, and then— *Dear God! What was that?*

David yelled out at the flash of unspeakable pleasure. It was no sooner over than it was back again, coinciding with the brush of Balfour's clever fingers inside him. Again and again Balfour touched him like that, till David was whimpering and pleading incoherently. And then, finally, with one last deep, internal caress, and his hot mouth imprisoning David's rigid flesh, Balfour brought David to an orgasm like no other he'd ever experienced.

David cried out, bowing his back, his cock pulsing as he emptied his balls into the other man's mouth. He glanced down, almost coming again when he saw Balfour's strong throat muscles working as he swallowed David's spend, the pale gold breadth of his perfect shoulders crowding between David's spread thighs.

David sagged back against the pillows, feeling utterly boneless; he was unable to do anything but watch as Balfour rose to his knees, bracing one fist on the pillow next to David's head, and taking himself in hand. His arm moved in a blur as he worked himself, his gaze fixed on David's face, his mouth set almost in a snarl. Mere moments later, his own climax was shooting out, coating David's chest and belly with his seed before Balfour collapsed on top of him, panting.

For a minute, they lay there, Balfour's spend cooling between them, his hot breath in David's ear.

David didn't know what to do next. He'd never lain in bed with a man before. Had never been fully naked with anyone like this.

After a bit, Balfour moved away, extricating himself from their tangled limbs and flopping down onto his back beside David. David felt oddly bereft. He stared at the ceiling rose while the reality of what he'd just allowed began to slowly dawn on him. He couldn't bear to look at Balfour though he felt the man's gaze on him.

He waited for Balfour to speak, to break the silence with one of his provoking comments, but instead, Balfour sat up and swung his legs off the bed. Standing up, he crossed to the sideboard to pour water from a jug into the ewer. Taking a washcloth, he cleaned his hands and groin. When he was finished, he wet another cloth and brought it to David, handing it to him expressionlessly.

"You're welcome to stay the night," Balfour said, donning a dressing gown as David cleaned up. David felt sure the invitation wasn't genuine. The offer was spoken politely, as though Balfour was offering tea to an uninvited guest. A hollow feeling began to grow in David's gut.

"Thank you, but it's time I left." He sat up, searching the floor for a few moments with his eyes before he realised his clothes were all in the sitting room. *Christ.* Nothing for it but to get up and walk across the room naked.

Steeling himself, he got up and made his way into the sitting room, where he began to pick up his crumpled clothes. Eventually he became aware of Balfour lounging in the doorway between the two rooms, silently watching David dress. A strange tension seemed to vibrate off him.

"At least admit you enjoyed it," Balfour said after a while, his tone faintly hostile.

David looked up from fastening his breeches. "I never said otherwise."

That didn't seem to mollify Balfour at all. He stared balefully at the floor.

"What's wrong?" David asked quietly. He wondered if the other man had resented David's lack of active participation. Generally, David tended to do most of the work in his encounters, but tonight he'd lain back and let Balfour do everything.

"Nothing's wrong," Balfour snapped.

David's hands stilled. He waited. He'd cross-examined enough witnesses to know a pregnant silence when he heard one.

"It's just that—" Balfour looked up and fastened that dark

gaze on David again. He was scowling. "I find I still want you."

Unsure what to say, David stayed silent, watching Balfour warily.

"It's like a sickness," Balfour continued. "Ever since I met you. You've been…preying on my mind. It's irritating. I never entertain repeat performances."

"I see."

Balfour gave a harsh laugh. "Do you?"

David shrugged. "You thought we'd have this, and the itch would be gone." He understood that delusion. In the past, after every encounter he had with another man, he'd make promises to himself that it would never happen again. *Just this once.*

Balfour stared at him, his gaze very cold. "An itch. Is that what you call it?"

"Well, what do you call it?" David shot back, retrieving his cravat from the floor and looping it about his neck.

"I've never thought about it before tonight," Balfour said tightly. "Desire, I suppose. More than an *itch*, anyway."

David's hands stilled in the midst of tying his cravat and he stared at the other man, his heart thudding. Balfour stood and glared back. He was such a contradiction, speaking those oddly flattering words in such a cold, almost affronted manner. As though he thought David had done something underhanded to make him feel that way.

After a long, tense pause, David shifted his gaze and reached for his evening coat. "We agree on one thing at least," he said mildly as he shouldered it on. "Repeat performances are a bad idea."

He was aware of Balfour regarding him silently for a moment while he buttoned his coat; then the larger man stalked across the room and pulled the servants' bell.

"We agree on something else," Balfour bit out. "It's time you left."

The sudden aggression in his tone drew David's attention, and he saw that there was a tightness to Balfour's jaw, a thinness to his generous mouth, that spoke of barely controlled anger.

David silently bent to fetch his shoes. By the time he was finished dressing, a footman was knocking at the door. Balfour opened it and stood aside to display the waiting servant. He didn't look at David. "Johnston will see you out," he said.

David walked to the door, pausing a moment to look at Balfour as he left. He felt he should say something—as though he'd regret it forever if he didn't speak—but his throat felt oddly constricted, and he didn't know what it was he wanted to say anyway. So in the end he just gave a jerky nod and went. The door closed behind him with a decisive click.

David followed the footman down the corridor, his mind teeming with thoughts. Why the hell had Balfour been so angry? David had given Balfour everything he'd wanted, hadn't he? Allowed things he'd never allowed anyone else. The new, fierce memory of what they'd done together hit David like a physical blow: Balfour's head bent over David's cock, his fingers moving inside David's body, his face as he stroked his own cock, clenched in agonised pleasure—

Oh God.

The way David had come. So hard, so unrestrained. Yelling out his pleasure.

David glanced at the footman as they descended the staircase. Had he heard David crying out? The sudden horror of that thought made David's gorge rise.

God in heaven, what had he *done*?

When they reached the hallway, the footman fetched David's greatcoat and hat. David allowed the man to help him on with the greatcoat, his shame and mortification growing all the time.

Then, at last, the footman was opening the door, politely

inclining his head. As soon as the gap was wide enough, David shoved his way out. He couldn't wait to leave Balfour's house. He welcomed the bruising glance of his shoulder against the wood of the doorframe. The pain distracted him for a moment from the turmoil in his mind.

Once he was out, he didn't look back. He practically fell down the steps to the street below in his hurry to leave and started running. He ran along Queen Street, streaking past serried ranks of identical townhouses, turning off to pound up the steep hill of Hanover Street. When he crested the hill at George Street, his heart felt ready to burst out of his chest. Still he ran. Across Princes Street and all the way up the Mound. Farther, till he reached the bottom of Fleshmarket Close. Only then did he stop, at the foot of that steep alleyway, to bend over, panting and half retching, sick with exhaustion and regret.

Once he had his breath back, he slowly straightened and looked into the darkness of the close. He never came this way at night, though it was a shortcut home. The close was unlit and black as hell. He could hear the panting curses of a man fucking a whore up against the wall. When he stepped into it, when the gloom swallowed him up like the maw of a great beast, the stink of piss and ale and sour fear was overwhelming. A distant part of him knew he should turn back.

But he didn't.

Halfway up the close, once David was as far into the dark as he could be and with the stink near choking him, a man stepped out of the shadows.

"Gi'e us your coin."

The man's voice was thick with drink and thrummed with the threat of violence. David knew he should be afraid but he felt…nothing. The whole situation felt unreal, but some sort of response appeared to be required.

"I think not," he said, marvelling at how calm he sounded.

It was only when the man's hulking shadow shot forward

that the numbness dissipated. Fear exploded in David. His heart pounded and energy flooded his limbs. Time seemed to slow as he braced himself for the man's attack. But it was a blow from behind him that hit him first. Something stout and heavy that struck the back of his head. He staggered forward, just as the first man's fist came forward and hit his temple a glancing blow.

Even as David reeled, a strange calmness came over him, as though this had always been inevitable. As though it was right. Energy surged in him. All that mattered was this single struggle. He drew back his fist and punched the aggressor in front of him with everything he had. The jarring pain that travelled up his arm was almost as shocking as the pain in his head, but somehow he kept going, striking again and again, twisted satisfaction filling all the yawning spaces inside him when he heard someone grunt with pain. The brawl lasted only a minute—less. The end came with a second blow to the back of his head.

He dropped like a stone, the ground coming up to meet him, cold and hard beneath his cheek. Hands rifled over him, and a vicious boot caught him twice in the ribs, making him groan and curl in on himself.

And then he was left, stunned and bleeding on the wet cobbles.

CHAPTER TWELVE

One of the whores helped David up. She sat him on her stoop till he came round and gave him a nip of gin. She made him lean on her while he walked up to the top of the close. Her name was Janet, his mother's name, and she looked about the same age.

His money had been stolen, along with his watch. He told Janet he'd come back with a coin for her in thanks another day. Janet just snorted and waved him on. "Away ye go and get tae bed."

It wasn't far to his rooms, and he managed to weave his way dazedly home without further incident. He staggered inside, lit a candle and washed the blood from his face and the back of his head, which was now pounding. He felt tired and shaky, not even up to undressing. He lay down on the bed in his clothes and fell into a deep, dreamless sleep.

The next day, he awoke feeling like hell. There was a crust of dried blood on the back of his head, which felt sore and tender. When he looked in the mirror, he discovered that half his face was grazed from his fall to the ground and he had a black eye. It hurt when he breathed in. What had possessed him to walk through Fleshmarket Close last night?

It was a question he asked himself over and over, and at the back of his mind, an answer lurked, one he didn't want to examine too closely. A morbid desire for oblivion had suffused him last night, carrying his feet forward into a darkness he had known to be dangerous. He hadn't cared in that moment what would happen to him.

He hurt in a different way when he thought about the events at Balfour's house. Removing his stiff, dirty clothes, he had to banish memories of Balfour undoing his buttons, unwinding his neckcloth, pulling his shirt over his head. He tried to push the memory of that slow undressing to the back of his mind, but the pictures were still there. As was the ghost of Balfour's mouth kissing him, Balfour's big, warm body pressing against his own.

Years of keeping his encounters with other men as anonymous and impersonal as possible had gone to hell last night. He'd broken all his own rules. He'd gone to Balfour's home, laid in his bed, kissed him, allowed the man to penetrate him intimately. Even now the thought of it had his gut clenching and regret washing over him. But Christ, it had felt so good. Far too good.

"I never entertain repeat performances."

And neither did David.

Once David was naked, he examined himself. His torso was badly bruised. If he'd been at home, his mother would have wrapped it in coarse paper soaked in vinegar. For a moment, he wondered if he should do that, but he was sure he didn't have the right sort of paper. In the end, he merely donned a nightshirt and went back to bed, where he spent most of Sunday, sleeping on and off, emerging only once to unearth some food. While he slept, his dreams looped anxiously—missed hearings, mislaid papers, looking for something, looking for someone. He'd feared he'd dream of Balfour, but he didn't—not once. It was only his waking hours that were haunted by the man.

Whenever he thought of what he'd done with Balfour, his prick swelled, even as regret suffused him. Twice he took himself in hand and brought himself to completion at the memories. Both times he was swamped by bitter regret after.

He felt better on Monday, though his bruises and grazes possibly looked worse. His maidservant, Ellen, arrived early and cried out when she saw his face. "What happened to you, Mr. Lauriston?"

"It's nothing," he said. "I was foolish enough to take a shortcut home on Saturday and was lucky only to suffer a few bruises and a stolen watch."

"Oh, but your bonny face, sir!"

She made him sit while she examined him. "I've brought your breakfast, but you've not a thing else in the place—as usual." She always scolded him like this, even though she was several years his junior.

"You know I usually eat my meals out."

"Aye, well, you'll no' be out today, will you? I'll go and get you some food, and when I come back, I'll bring you some good ointment for that bruisin'."

Within half an hour, she'd laid a new fire, swept and tidied his sitting room and set down his breakfast—two kippers and butter. Then she took the coins he gave her and departed while he ate. He hadn't thought he was hungry, but he ate both kippers and mopped up all the butter with his bread. He felt much better after his meal, and while the maid-servant was gone, he shaved and dressed himself properly.

"You look better already," she declared with satisfaction when she returned, but she still made him sit again and applied her ointment to his bruises.

He stayed at home all day, immersing himself in reading for the case he and Chalmers were working on and trying to banish all thoughts of Saturday's events from his mind. Ellen stocked his meagre larder and cleaned his rooms during the morning, taking a bundle of laundry away with her when she left and promising to have it back when she came again on Wednesday. For the rest of the day, he was alone.

He managed well enough till evening came. He'd slept so much the day before that he wasn't tired at all, but his head still ached and his concentration was poor. Eventually he abandoned his work and tried to read the *Edinburgh Review* instead, but it was to no avail. All he could think about was his behaviour with Balfour. He'd allowed Balfour to touch him more intimately than any person ever had before, and when he thought of where the man had put his mouth, his fingers—

David dropped his head into his hands and squeezed his eyes tightly shut. However ashamed he might feel now, he wouldn't tell himself lies. He had willingly let go of his reservations and allowed Balfour to do things to him he had sworn to himself he would never allow. And when he remembered the sensations that had racked his body as Balfour had worked him—as he'd sucked David's cock and penetrated him with his fingers in skilful counterpoint—it made David want to experience it all again.

"No," he moaned aloud, his head still cradled in his hands. But no matter his feelings now, it had happened. It had. One of those carefully tended fences of his had been breached forever.

He stood and went into the kitchen. On the top shelf of the larder, he kept his whisky. He took it down, poured a generous dram and threw it straight down his throat. Snatching up both bottle and glass, he headed back to the sitting room, sat down and began to drink in earnest, chasing oblivion.

An hour later, with more than half the bottle gone, he finally fell asleep in his chair, the glass tumbled, forgotten, to the floor.

On Tuesday, David ventured to the faculty library. He had little choice. He and Chalmers were meeting the solicitor in the MacAllister case at eleven o'clock. The hearing was in a few weeks. David had meticulously reviewed all the papers and witness precognitions again to identify the weakest areas of their case and suggest how the gaps might be filled. He was to sit down with Chalmers at nine o'clock to take him through his conclusions.

"What happened to you?" Chalmers asked when David approached him in the library. The man's eyebrows were raised—that was about as dramatic a reaction as it was possible to get from Chalmers.

"Thieves. My own fault. I took a shortcut home on Saturday night through a dark close."

"Not the brightest idea you've ever had," Chalmers concurred. "Are you all right?"

"I'll live."

With that, they got down to business.

They worked well together. Chalmers appreciated David's hard work, and David welcomed the older man's shrewd insights. Chalmers questioned some of David's conclusions about the case and made several additional suggestions David hadn't thought of which they debated vigorously. David grew animated as they discussed the case, his sharp mind dissecting Chalmers's arguments as he dealt with them point by point. He had always been able to rely on his work for this—to draw him out of himself; to help him forget his worries.

When the solicitor arrived for the consultation, Chalmers gave the man a list of tasks as long as his arm to carry out over the next two weeks before they consulted again. There would be little for David to do on the case before then, and he left the meeting feeling aimless.

He had several other cases, but not much was happening on any of them at present. He went to speak with his clerk, but there were no messages for him, and when he checked his box again, it was empty.

He felt low when he left the library, and without any conscious decision to do so, took a detour on the way home to buy another bottle of whisky. He drank half of it with his scanty dinner, falling into a mercifully dreamless sleep in front of the fire.

By Wednesday, he still hadn't heard anything from Euan, and the lad's silence had begun to bother him. David hadn't liked how Euan had been talking on Saturday night as they watched the entrance to the Assembly Rooms from their dark close. Following Isabella Galbraith. Watching for Lees. In one evening, his plan had escalated into something new and infinitely more dangerous.

Midmorning, David went to the library, where he made himself speak to a few of the senior advocates. Then he spent an hour in a coffee house, trying to read a newspaper before heading down Fleshmarket Close. It was his third visit since the attack, and this time he found his quarry—Janet the whore. He pressed a half crown into her hand, waved off her garbled thanks and took his leave.

He decided then that it would do no harm to take a turn down to the New Town, to see if Euan was indeed there. He knew the Galbraiths lived on Heriot Row after all, and it wasn't as though he had anything better to do.

It was a cold but sunny autumn day, and David enjoyed the stroll. If he'd been at home on a day like this, striding down the country lanes near Midlauder, he'd have taken his hat and coat off, but that wasn't possible in the grand part of Edinburgh that was the New Town. Instead he had to content himself with tipping his head back and letting the sun shine directly on his face.

When he got to Heriot Row, he slowed his pace and began to carefully observe his surroundings but was unable to spot anything out of the ordinary. He was so busy looking for a young man loitering that he didn't notice the two ladies strolling towards him.

"Mr. Lauriston! What are you doing here?"

His head snapped up to see Elizabeth Chalmers and her sister Catherine approaching him, arm in arm.

"Miss Chalmers, Miss Catherine—" he began but broke off when he saw Elizabeth's expression. Her eyes were wide with horror.

"Oh my word, what *happened* to you?" she cried.

With an inward sigh, he pasted a smile upon his face and told the story he'd now told a dozen times all over again.

"Oh, you poor thing!" Elizabeth exclaimed when he was finished. "Did you have anyone to look after you?"

"I didn't need anyone—"

"Of course you do, everyone does!"

"Truly," he insisted. "It looks much worse than it is. My pride has taken the hardest blow. It was very foolish of me to go where I did."

Elizabeth opened her mouth to protest his waving away of her concern, but he beat her to it, asking brightly, "And where are you ladies off to on this lovely day?"

"We are on our way to call on Miss Galbraith," Catherine replied. "She lives on this very street."

"Oh, does she?" David replied, managing a creditable degree of polite surprise.

"Yes, at the other end," Catherine said, gesturing to where David had just come from. He thought quickly. At the very least, it would be good to see exactly where Miss Galbraith lived.

"Will you allow me to escort you both, then?" he asked, turning on his heel. "I really ought to return to Parliament House, and your company, if only for a few minutes, would make that a much more pleasant prospect."

Elizabeth beamed, and Catherine smiled politely. "That

would be lovely," Elizabeth said happily, curling her little hand round David's proffered arm.

They strolled slowly back down Heriot Row, making polite conversation. David tried to appear interested in the ladies' excitement over a lecture on phrenology they had attended while surreptitiously looking for any sign of Euan.

"Oh, look, Lizzie," Catherine suddenly said, interrupting her sister. "It is Lord Murdo *again!*"

David's heartbeat immediately quickened from an easy stroll to a full-blown gallop. He looked up and saw Balfour leaving a house only twenty yards away.

"You were right," Catherine continued, laughing. "This has to be more than mere friendship. Surely he means to ask Bella to marry him? He has been showing her such *particular* attentions."

"Kate, really!" Elizabeth chided. "It is quite wrong for you to talk so in front of Mr. Lauriston. He will be embarrassed!"

David made some automatic protest that he wasn't remotely embarrassed. At the very same moment, Balfour turned his head. Their gazes met, and Balfour looked briefly shocked at David's appearance, though he covered it quickly.

He waited for them to reach the house he had just left, greeting the ladies with a smile as they drew closer.

"Miss Chalmers and Miss Catherine, how nice to see you both again." He nodded at David. "Mr. Lauriston."

"Good afternoon, Lord Murdo," Elizabeth replied. "We are here to call on our friend, Miss Galbraith. I gather you have had the same notion."

"Indeed," Balfour said. "I am sure you will find her in very good health, as I did."

David decided it was time to retreat, preferably leaving Balfour with the ladies while he made good his escape. "Please do excuse me, Miss Chalmers, Miss Catherine. I must go if I am not to be late." He glanced at Balfour and gave the barest nod. "Lord Murdo."

"What happened to you, Lauriston?" Balfour demanded.

"Mr. Lauriston was attacked!" Catherine supplied before David could speak.

"Attacked?"

David opened his mouth to demur, but Elizabeth spoke before he could do so. "Yes! On the way home from the Assembly on Saturday! Isn't it too awful?"

Balfour said nothing. His expressionless gaze was pinned on David.

"It was nothing," David murmured. "Just a bit of foolishness on my part."

"Foolishness?"

David felt warmth steal over his cheeks. "I took an unwise shortcut late at night," he said, shrugging. "And paid the price, as you can see."

"Yes, I see."

There was a brief, awkward silence.

"I really must go," David said. He bowed over the ladies' hands and took his leave, promising to call on them soon at Elizabeth's urging. He felt sure he was going to get away alone, but Balfour moved away with him as the ladies climbed the steps to their friend's house.

"You look awful," Balfour said flatly once they were out of earshot.

David scowled and said nothing, quickening his step. Balfour merely picked up his own pace to keep abreast of him.

"Why were you so stupid as to take a shortcut so late at night?" Balfour demanded. "You strike me as an intelligent fellow."

David ignored him, but Balfour kept talking.

"Do you have a death wish? You could have been killed —" The man's voice was rising, inexplicable anger in his tone.

David ground to a halt, turning to face him with clenched fists and jaw. "What business is it of yours?" he bit out.

That brought Balfour up short. He faced David with equal belligerence, but though his gaze was angry—accusing, almost—he said nothing, pressing his lips together as though to stop any words emerging. David returned his stare for a long moment, then shook his head and turned on his heel. Somewhat to his surprise, Balfour followed.

The silence between them was oppressive, and after a while, David couldn't bear it any longer. He forced himself to be civil. Normal. As though the last few minutes had not taken place. "Did you find Miss Galbraith in good spirits?" he asked politely.

"Yes." Balfour paused, then added slyly, with a sidelong glance, "What did you make of her? She's very lovely, don't you think?"

David hesitated for a moment before agreeing. "Yes, very. Accomplished too, I'm sure. And well-bred."

Balfour looked straight ahead again. "Hmmm."

"All in all a perfect wife," David added coolly.

Balfour smiled without looking at David. It was a humourless, inward smile. A little bit hateful. "Do you seek to make a point, my friend?"

David realised then he couldn't pretend civility with Balfour. "I'm not your friend," he said.

Balfour's expression tightened, but he ignored David's comment. "Fancy Miss Galbraith for yourself, do you?"

David flushed. "You know that's not what I meant."

"What, then?"

"Catherine Chalmers just mentioned she believes you're about to ask for Miss Galbraith's hand in marriage."

Balfour huffed out a laugh. "And if I am?"

"Are you?"

"Perhaps. My father thinks she'd be an ideal wife for me. What do you think?"

David forced himself to shrug. "I have no idea, but I'll wish you happy, of course."

Balfour gave a bark of laughter. "How kind."

That laugh made David feel foolish and angry. He wanted to lash out at the other man. Tell him he wasn't fit to wed any woman. It took all his self-control to stay silent.

He felt Balfour's gaze on his face but kept looking resolutely ahead.

"Listen, I don't want—" Balfour began after a brief silence, only to break off, his step faltering suddenly.

David turned his head then, his own pace stuttering to a halt. There was perhaps a second—less—when Balfour stood still, staring across the road, eyes wide with surprise. And then, just as David looked in the direction of Balfour's gaze, Balfour set off at a run. He was already past David by the time David saw what it was that had gripped his attention: another man. Tall and soberly dressed. Walking smartly, then quickening to a run as Balfour shouted a name after him.

"*Hugh!*"

The man threw a glance over his shoulder as he disappeared round a corner, Balfour on his heels.

He could've been Balfour's brother.

CHAPTER THIRTEEN

A full day passed before David heard from Euan again. A full day during which David worried about the lad almost incessantly.

He was sure the man he'd seen Balfour chasing after must be Lees. If that was right, it meant Lees was here, in Edinburgh, just as Euan had always thought. And if Balfour had found him, on Isabella Galbraith's doorstep, might Euan have done so too? Might their confrontation already have taken place?

If so, what had become of Euan?

The lad had promised he would speak to David before he went after Lees, but it had been five days since David had seen him. Perhaps Euan had seen his quarry and given in to the temptation of facing up to him then and there? But he *had* promised not to do so, and David knew he was not one to make a promise lightly.

Although David had nothing pressing to work on, he went to the library after lunch to check if Euan had called on him there, or perhaps left a note in his box. But there was nothing, no message and no note. He went home again and tried to do some reading but couldn't concentrate at all. By late afternoon, he'd decided to take another walk down to Heriot Row to see if he could find the lad there. He was just about to put his on coat when there was a knock at his front door.

And there, at last, stood Euan.

He was filthy and his skin was grey from exhaustion, his eyes red-rimmed. He had lost weight—in just a handful of days, he had become noticeably thinner. David stood aside to let the lad pass, but Euan didn't move.

"I came to tell you I've found Lees," he said, jaw set, expression grim. "So there you go. Promise fulfilled." And with that he turned away, as if to go.

"Euan—wait." David reached for him, catching him by the arm and pulling him back. "Come in, for God's sake."

Euan stopped, but he didn't move. He stayed stock-still, resisting David's tug at his sleeve, and stared at the ground. "I have to go—I have things to do, Davy."

"You look terrible," David said gently. "Have you been sleeping? Come in and eat something. Rest for a bit."

"I can't. I—"

"Just for a little while. Please."

Euan stood rigid for a moment; then something in him seemed to give, and he turned. He looked weary to the very bone, as though he hadn't slept or eaten for a long while. "All right. I'll just come in for a bit, though."

David boiled eggs and toasted bread over the fire while Euan washed up. He was slathering the toast in butter when Euan came back into the kitchen, fair hair damp and beard all scraped away, one of David's clean shirts on his back.

"Go and sit in the other room in front of the fire," David said brusquely. "Take this with you." He thrust a pewter tankard of ale into the younger man's hand.

"You're always feeding me," the lad said.

"You need to be fed. Go."

After a pause, Euan obeyed, his gait stiff.

David dished the food onto a plate and poured a glass of whisky for himself, then followed Euan into the sitting room. The lad had settled into a winged armchair in front of the fire, and his eyelids were drooping already. David had to call his name softly to rouse him before he was able to hand the meal over and take a chair on the other side of the fire.

Euan ate the food quickly without uttering another word. He broke the tops off the eggs, fingers trembling, and scooped out the creamy insides, washing it all down with the ale.

"Good?" David asked when he was done, topping up his own glass.

Euan nodded. "Aye. It's been a while since I last ate."

"Or slept, by the look of you."

Euan gave a soft, humourless laugh, which David took as an affirmation.

"So, you came to tell me you've found Lees?"

"I promised to tell you before I faced him, didn't I?" There was an edge of resentment in his tone.

"Yes, and I'm glad you did," David said gravely. "How did you find him?"

Euan leaned his head back against the chair and closed his eyes. "It all went to plan. I followed the girl to her home on Saturday night, then set about finding a place to watch the house from."

"Where?"

"One of the nearby houses is empty." His mouth stretched into a sneering sort of smile, eyes still closed. "Rich people who live in London most of the time."

David was taken aback by his bitter tone but kept his own voice neutral. "You broke in?"

"No, it's locked up fast as you like. I just climbed over the railings and sheltered in front of the kitchen door."

"Outside? Christ man, it's been raining on and off all week and bloody freezing besides!"

"It wasn't so bad. The steps to the front door sheltered me from the rain, and I had my coat to sleep in."

"Just a coat? Euan, you could've frozen to death!"

"There's plenty have worse," Euan replied, opening his eyes and settling his cool gaze on David. "Plenty. Are you getting so used to fancy folk you don't see that anymore?"

"Of course not," David protested, but he knew there was an element of truth in Euan's slur. When David had first come to the city, he'd been shocked by the widespread poverty. Now he was inured to it all—the beggars, the prostitutes, the dirty, ragged poor of the city. He walked by them every day and, for the most part, ignored their pleas. It was impossible to do otherwise if you were to get on with life. Impossible to help everyone. Anyone.

"It wasn't so bad," Euan continued. "I had a good hiding place to watch from and catch up on my sleep when I couldn't stay awake any longer. It took a few days, but eventually, today, he came. Like he was answering my prayers."

"It's definitely him?"

"Aye. I'd know him anywhere. He looks like that other one, from the assembly, but you wouldn't mistake either of them for the other, once you see them properly. They're alike, but not *that* alike." He smiled then, almost dreamily. "I followed him when he came out from visiting his lass. I was that tired and hungry, Davy, and it felt like he'd never stop walking. But eventually he went back to where he's staying. You should see it. It calls itself a hotel but it's nothing better than a whore's den, from what I seen."

"So now you know where he lives."

"That I do. I came straight here after. I meant to tell you and go back without waiting. But—" He broke off.

"But?"

Euan dropped his head back against the chair, and his

eyelids fell again, purplish and puffy from lack of sleep. "I was so tired..." He sighed.

"You were right to stop," David said, his voice low and soothing. "You needed to eat and rest. No one can keep going so long without food or sleep."

By the time David had finished his short speech, Euan had dropped off, his jaw slackening, mouth falling open to let out the slow, regular breaths of sleep. He was gone so suddenly, so thoroughly, he must've been tired enough to fall asleep standing up.

David refilled his whisky glass.

He sat in his armchair and watched the younger man sleep for a long time, while the logs in the fireplace burned down to white ash and the spirit in the bottle dwindled.

He was relieved Euan had come to him, that he had this chance to talk with the lad before the confrontation. He'd never be able persuade Euan to give up on his quest to face up to Lees, but he could at least go with him. Lees wouldn't be able to dispatch two of them, he hoped.

In his heart of hearts, David hadn't believed it would ever come to this. Euan's plan had seemed hopeless to him at the beginning. Unlikely. God, but he regretted that arrogance. Not only had he been wrong, he'd become pivotal to Euan's plan. It was David who had found Isabella Galbraith. David who had been the means of Euan locating his quarry.

If Lees harmed Euan—killed him even—David would be responsible.

"Why does everythin' have to be black or white, wi' you, son?"

That was what his mother used to say to him after he fought with the old man.

"Ye're just like each other. Unbendin' as bloody oak trees."

Was he unbending?

What was it Balfour had called him? *An idealist.*

That sounded better, but it meant the same thing, didn't

it? An absolutist? A man so wedded to his principles he couldn't accept there were shades of grey?

No, that wasn't it. David knew very well there were shades of grey. He just didn't feel they applied to him. For good or ill, he'd never been able to give himself an easy way out. And he wouldn't now.

If Euan was harmed on this wild quest of his, it would be on David's soul.

CHAPTER FOURTEEN

It was his neck that woke him.

A deep pain. David stirred and winced, the ache sharp when he moved the head that had lolled awkwardly as he slept.

He'd fallen asleep in his chair. Had he been drinking again?

The candles had burned down while he was unconscious. Now the only light came from a ghost of a fire in the grate. Its weak glow touched the edges of the furniture, just enough for David to make out the terrain of the room.

In the time it took him to shift in his chair, blink his eyes and assess the state of his head—clear and pain-free; he couldn't have drunk that much—he remembered. Opening the door to Euan. Feeding him and listening to him.

David's eyes shifted to the other armchair. He wasn't surprised to see it was empty but still cursed under his breath. He hadn't intended to sleep. He hadn't even thought he was particularly tired. His own fault, though, for drinking and allowing his eyes to close.

Levering himself out of his chair, he called the other man's name, though without much hope of a reply. Silence greeted his efforts.

He went to the sideboard, grunting aloud when he bumped his hip painfully into the sharp edge of the table on the way. Once there, he fiddled around for a candle, eventually finding a half-used one. Straightening the wick of the candle stub to a smooth point, he crossed to the fireplace and held it to the white-hot embers to light it. The wick flared, then dimmed a little as he turned the stub upright. The flame flickered from the persistent draught in the room, and David had to guard it with his curved left hand as he checked his rooms. There was no sign of Euan.

In the last room, the bedchamber, he sat down and let out a long sigh. He had no doubt that Euan had gone to face up to Lees. Now David would have to go after him, and at night too.

He washed his face in cold water to wake himself up and pulled his boots on as he considered what to do. What was it Euan told him before he fell asleep? That Lees was staying in a hotel? But which one? He didn't have so much as a vague direction to go on.

David racked his brains, but all he could come up with was that Balfour might know. Balfour had run after Lees—or *Hugh*, as he'd called him—that last time David had seen him. If Balfour had caught up with Hugh, perhaps he knew where the man was now.

It wasn't much to go on, but it was all David had.

As David shrugged into his coat, he calculated how long it would take to run to Balfour's house on Queen Street, knock on his door and beg for his help. No matter how quick, and even assuming Balfour would be there, it would be too long. Euan might be an hour ahead of David already and knew exactly where Lees was. But what else could he do? It was this or stay at home and wait for news, and *that* he could not do. With no time to waste, David jammed his hat on and left his rooms, setting a path for Balfour's house.

Despite his concerns about time, he avoided shortcuts, sticking to the better-lit and safer streets. Even these were dim tonight. The *haar*—the cold Edinburgh mist, straight off the sea—had drifted in, and the already dim street lanterns glowed weakly through the ghostly murk. David couldn't see more than a few feet in front of him. Nevertheless, he ran, settling into a steady pace that he knew he could keep up over several miles.

It wasn't long before he was mounting the steps to Balfour's house, his breath sawing in and out of his chest. He battered on the glossy door with his fist, taking gulps of air as he waited for an answer.

More than a minute passed. He wondered whether he was going to be ignored and set about a second round of battering, but at last the door opened a crack, and the same footman David had seen on his last visit poked his head out.

"May I help you," he asked frostily, evincing no sign of recognition.

"I need to see Lord Murdo," David replied.

"Regretfully, his lordship is not at home." There was no regret in the man's gaze, though, rather a superior sort of satisfaction. He was the type that enjoyed refusing people.

And David didn't believe him. He *couldn't*.

"I'm quite sure if you ask him, he will agree to see me," David insisted, moving forward to cross the threshold, his body almost touching the other man now. "Tell him it's Mr. Lauriston, if you please. And that it's urgent." Surprised by David's sudden assertiveness, the footman stepped backwards momentarily, giving up valuable ground and allowing David to insinuate himself farther into the house. Just as quickly, though, he regrouped, drawing himself up to his full height and barring entrance to the house by bracing his arm against the doorframe.

"Kindly stand back—"

But David refused to retreat. He ducked his head under the footman's arm and shouted, "Balfour! Balfour, I must see you!"

The footman cursed and brought his arm down, trying to secure David under one burly arm while David tried to thrash out of his grip and shouted for Balfour again.

A voice rang out from upstairs. "What on earth is going on?"

Decisive footsteps descended.

David stilled, letting himself be held. "Balfour, it's David Lauriston," he said loudly. "I need to speak to you."

The feet that made those footsteps—shod in Turkish slippers—were the first thing David actually saw of Balfour, caught as he was, head down, under the footman's arm. He craned his neck up and found his quarry looking as amused as ever to find him thus secured.

"I have to speak with you," David said angrily.

"Is that so?" Balfour said. His eyes gleamed, and a smile ghosted over his lips. Then, to Johnston, "Let him go, you dolt."

Abruptly, the meaty arm holding David loosened. "I told the gentleman you weren't at home, my lord," the footman said apologetically. "But he wouldn't listen!"

David straightened, dusting himself down. He hated that he must be red-faced and sweating now. "Since Lord Murdo *is* home," he bit out, "I'm not sure why you're complaining."

"He was following orders," Balfour said flatly. He turned to his servant, adding wearily, "For God's sake, Johnston, shut the door."

While the footman hurried to do his bidding, Balfour glanced at David. "Follow me."

David did as he was bid, shadowing the man down the corridor. Balfour was dressed in an ornate dressing gown, a beautiful thing of pale gold silk with wide black silk cuffs and black embroidery. Luxurious and incomparable. It looked like the sort of garment that should be worn by an emperor or a pasha. It didn't belong here, in this cold, northern city. Much like Balfour himself.

Balfour led David into a well-lit library. Evidently he'd been working on something at his desk—it was strewn with papers. A half-drunk glass of port sat beside a pile of ledgers.

Balfour took up his seat behind the desk again and gestured to David to take the smaller chair on the other side, putting him in the position of a petitioner. Well, he couldn't really complain; he *was* a petitioner, after all. Or was about to be.

"So, Lauriston, what do you want?" Balfour leaned back in his chair, half smiling, his dark gaze steady.

David took a deep breath. "I hardly know where to start," he began.

"Goodness me! David Lauriston stumped for words? Now that does surprise me."

David stared at him, taken aback by Balfour's words, or rather by the faint sneer underlying them. Balfour returned his look with no more than a raised eyebrow.

"All right, then," David said after a long pause. "I'll get straight to the point, if I may. The other day, after I met you outside Miss Galbraith's home, you saw a man in the street, and you ran after him. I think I know who that man is." At Balfour's frown, he shrugged. "That is to say, I don't know *precisely* who he is, but I believe he's a government agent."

Despite how provocative that statement was, Balfour's expression didn't change much at all. One eyebrow lifted, by the smallest degree. Nothing more.

"I see," he said at length. "Pray, go on."

"He is, in fact, the man I spoke of on the night we dined with the Chalmers. The man who infiltrated the weavers' ranks. The man who brought about the events that resulted in all those executions and transportations."

Balfour's gaze was steady. "Is that right?"

"It is. And he is—at this very moment—being pursued by a man with revenge in mind."

Balfour's gaze sharpened, his studied unconcern dissipating. "You?"

The question took David so much by surprise that he started. "No, of course not!"

"Then who?"

"A friend of mine. A brother of one of the transported men. He came to me to ask me to help him find this man. And, somewhat unwittingly, I did."

Balfour frowned. "You helped him unwittingly?"

"My friend approached me weeks ago, telling me that the man he was looking for was in love with a young woman whose father I might know. He thought the young woman was the key to finding this man—I thought he was being naïve. I was certain that no agent of the Crown would be so foolish as to disclose secrets about himself that would enable him to be so easily found." David sighed. "I agreed to help him because I thought that, when he ultimately failed, as I was sure he would do, he would return to his studies."

"But?"

David grimaced. "But the woman was real, and she *was* key to finding him. And now my friend knows where he is."

"The woman was Isabella Galbraith," Balfour supplied, expressionless.

"Yes."

"And your friend is the young man from the assembly."

David said nothing.

Balfour stared at him for a long moment. "Why are you here?"

"I made my friend promise that if he found the man he sought—Lees was the name he went by—he would speak to me before he did anything. He was reluctant, but he promised. Today he came to me and fulfilled that promise.

Now he is free to act." David paused, looking away. "I hadn't intended to let him confront Lees without me, but—we both fell asleep, and when I woke, he was gone." He flushed then, realising how that confession sounded.

A muscle twitched in Balfour's jaw. "And now?"

"I fear my friend will be harmed. I came to you hoping you would be able to give me Lees's direction. I have to go after Euan. He has no idea what he's dealing with—"

"Why are you doing this?"

David gazed at the man, nonplussed. "I don't want him to be harmed. He's just a lad. Innocent."

Balfour's lip curled. "You are infatuated with him."

David shook his head, staring at the man lounging before him in disbelief. "I am asking you to help me save him. I fear for his life, Balfour. I don't need much—just an address. I'll go there myself."

"Don't you think you're overreacting?"

"No, I don't," David snapped. "The man Euan is going to confront incited men to do things that resulted in them being executed. What might he do to a hot-headed boy who faces up to him?"

Balfour's dark eyes moved over David's face, searching for something. Whether he found it or not, David did not know. After a moment, Balfour slowly turned in his chair and reached for the servants' bell. A footman soon appeared. Not Johnston this time.

"Have the carriage brought round," Balfour ordered. "I will be ready in five minutes; then Mr. Lauriston and I will be leaving for the Imperial Hotel."

The Imperial Hotel was several miles away, near Holyrood. Balfour's carriage made short work of the journey, and as they travelled, he gave David a potted history of the man David thought of as Lees—Balfour's cousin, it turned out.

"Hugh is the son of my father's youngest sister. She eloped with a redcoat before she was officially out—my father was furious—but the marriage was certainly fruitful. Hugh is one of seven. However, my uncle is far from wealthy, and Hugh always knew he'd have to make his own way in the world. I think he was happy enough about it, till he met Isabella Galbraith."

"He fell in love with her?" David asked.

"So he told me, when I finally caught up with him the other day."

"You didn't know before then?"

"I've been half courting her myself. I wouldn't have done that if I'd known." Balfour sounded indignant at the idea.

"So how did he come to spy on the weavers?"

Balfour said nothing for several long beats of time. Then softly he uttered, "My father."

"Your father?"

"My father is the most ruthless and ambitious man you could ever hope to meet." Balfour sighed. "What the purpose of all his intrigue is, I've never been able to understand, but it's what he lives for. He sees everyone as a pawn in his game. He's used me in the past, but I don't allow it anymore. He really ought to have been one of those great Elizabethan men, poisoning courtiers and plotting regicide. He'd have loved that."

"As it is, he's had to lower himself to transporting weavers?"

Balfour shot him a steady gaze. "That's about the size of it. My father's part of the inner circle of government. The government sees radicals as a threat and has been using agents to flush out the most dedicated ones.

"Hugh approached my father about Isabella Galbraith more than a year ago. He knew her father and mine were close friends, and he hoped my father would speak up for him with Isabella's parents. He was also hoping my father would find him a lucrative position in government. My father did neither. Instead he recruited Hugh into this game." Balfour laughed then, though without humour. "And he said nothing to Isabella's father. I suspect when Hugh drew her virtues to my father's attention, my father decided that she would make *me* an ideal wife. It was his idea I court her."

"Did you know Hugh was working for your father?"

"I found out a few months ago, from my aunt. She came to see me and begged me to find Hugh. She wanted to get him away from my father's influence. She guessed he was embroiled in something dangerous but didn't know what."

"So you came up from London to find him?"

"It's why I was in Stirling the first night I met you."

David felt his face flush scarlet at the vivid memory of that night and was glad of the shadowed carriage interior.

"And did you find him there?"

"No. I hadn't seen him for months when I caught sight of him on the street last week. He led me a merry dance, I can tell you, before I finally ran him to ground."

"And when you did?"

Balfour said nothing for several moments, and David couldn't make out his expression in the dark. "We didn't part well," he said at last. "Hugh wants to believe in my father. He wants to believe all this hasn't been for nothing. That he'll get his Bella, in the end."

The carriage drew to a halt before David could question Balfour further—they had reached the Imperial Hotel. Balfour made no immediate move, but reached inside his greatcoat and drew something out.

"Here."

He presented a knife to David, the blade pointing at his own breast, the hilt at David.

David frowned. "I don't want that," he said, shaking his

head. "Or need it."

Balfour made an impatient noise. "Don't be a fool. You've said you fear this confrontation may turn violent, *ergo* you may need to defend yourself. I have one of my own and a pistol too."

David's gaze jerked up to Balfour's face. The man looked grim but resolute. He was right, and David knew it, but the thought of violence sickened him.

"If you wish, you can wait here," Balfour added. "I don't mind going in there alone. I'd prefer it, actually."

David flushed with shame. He reached out and took the knife. He hadn't paused to find his gloves before he came out, and the steel hilt felt cold against his fingers. He weighed the blade in his hand. When he was a boy, he'd always had a knife on him. He used it every day in his work about the farm, for a hundred and one tasks. He'd never considered using it against another human being.

"Don't be ridiculous," he bit out. "Of course I'm going in. If anything, you should be the one to wait in the carriage. This was my idea, after all." He bent over and slid the knife into his boot.

"Be careful—" Balfour began.

"I know how to handle a knife!" David snapped, exasperated, jerking upright again.

Balfour stared at him for a moment, and the corner of his mouth slowly hitched. "I beg your pardon," he said at last. "Shall we go, then?"

David nodded stiffly, and Balfour tapped the roof of the carriage with his cane. The coachman pulled back the grille, and Balfour instructed him to wait for them round the corner.

As the carriage rumbled away over the cobbled lane, the horses' hooves clipping at a decorous and stately pace, David cast his eye over the building. The Imperial Hotel did not live up to its grand name. High and narrow, the grey walls boasted only a few small windows. The roof was topped with steep, crow-stepped gables, little staircases that led up to empty sky. This structure was a creature of the Old Town. No hint of classicism here. No columns, no arches, but all higgledy-piggledy steps and stairs, and the windows placed only where needed.

"Come on." Balfour's voice interrupted David's reverie. The bigger man was already walking to the front door, and David had to hurry to catch him up.

Balfour rapped on the stout wood with his silver-topped cane in sharp staccato.

The door was finally opened, after a second round of rapping, by a bad-tempered-looking fellow whose demeanour transformed to one of obsequious good humour when Balfour gave him a coin and drew him aside. Balfour handed over several more coins during their murmured conversation, in return, David presumed, for information and, ultimately, the fellow's departure through the very door he'd opened to them.

"He's making himself scarce for half an hour," Balfour explained at David's look of enquiry. "Come on. I'm told Hugh's room is on the third floor. Number twenty. Our friend doesn't know if he's in or not, so we'd better approach quietly. I'd like to have some idea of what I'm going to be walking in on, if possible."

They climbed two sets of rickety stairs and found themselves in a cramped, poorly lit corridor. One candle flickered, ready to gutter out, by the look of it, in a sconce on the wall. The rooms up here were smaller and closer together than on the floors below, the ceilings lower. Balfour placed his forefinger against his lips, and David nodded, but despite their best efforts at silence, their booted feet inevitably made some noise on the worn floorboards.

Halfway down the corridor, they reached a room with the number twenty painted on the rough wood. From inside came the rumble of angry voices. Hugh was clearly not alone, but it was difficult to make out words. The building might look ramshackle, but the walls and doors were thick enough. Balfour pressed his ear against the wood and listened for a few moments, then pulled back, a concerned frown drawing his brows.

"We have to go in," he whispered.

David's heart raced faster, his breath growing short and shallow. He stepped forward and pressed his own ear to the door, straining to make out what had made Balfour look so worried. There was no talking, but he heard an unmistakable grunt of pain and reared back, as though burned, shooting an alarmed glance at Balfour.

"Our friend told me the locks are feeble," Balfour murmured. "He suggested a determined assault on the door if we had to get in."

"You can't be serious," David hissed. "The door looks very stout."

"I was assured otherwise," Balfour whispered back. "And what else can we do?"

David bit his lip. Balfour was right.

"Get ready to come in straight after me," Balfour whispered, pressing himself up against the opposite wall to give himself as much of a run up as possible. It would only be a couple of strides, but Balfour was a big, burly man after all. He put his hand in his pocket and drew out his pistol, nodding at David's boot. David reluctantly bent and pulled out the knife.

Ready? Balfour mouthed.

David swallowed and nodded, heart pounding.

Then Balfour charged.

CHAPTER FIFTEEN

Balfour's shoulder struck the door, the heft of his big body slamming into it. With a loud splintering sound, the door gave way and flew inwards, smacking into the wall on the other side as Balfour rushed in, David on his heels.

The two occupants of the room jerked round to look at the invaders, the flash of shock across each face for a moment identical. There was half an instant of perfect stillness when David's mind struggled to take in the picture before him. It was all wrong. Euan was no victim here. He was standing tall and aiming a pistol at the other man, who was kneeling some distance away. The kneeling man—as large and powerfully built as Balfour—wore only a nightshirt, his hands interlaced behind his head. There was a cut at his temple that oozed blood and the early bloom of several bruises on his face.

David's gaze shifted to Euan. He looked almost as bad as he had a few hours ago as he'd stood at David's door. His coat was filthy from sleeping on the ground, his face shadowed with weariness, but something held him upright—the same thing that made his eyes burn with conviction as he considered David and Balfour.

"Murdo—"

This was from the captive. His eyes were wet, his expression slack with relief.

"Keep your eyes on me," Euan snapped, and the man turned his head back.

Balfour took one slow step forward. He held his pistol away from his body, pointing the muzzle at the floor.

"If you take another step, I'll blow his head off," Euan said flatly.

Balfour stilled. "All right," he said, his deep voice even and slow. "We only want to talk to you."

Euan gave a short, humourless laugh. "Is that so? That's just what we've been doing, haven't we, Lees? Having a nice talk about how you betrayed my brother and all his friends."

Hugh closed his eyes and swallowed, the momentary relief from seeing Balfour all washed away.

"Euan, listen to me—" David began. The knife felt wrong in his hand.

"I said don't move," the younger man shouted, even though David hadn't shifted. "Don't take another step, Davy, or I swear—" He broke off, incoherent.

Balfour's hand landed heavily on David's shoulder. "Careful," he murmured.

"Why did you come here?" Euan exclaimed. His eyes went briefly to Balfour before he returned his gaze to the kneeling man. "And with *him* of all people?"

"I needed his help to find you," David replied. "I came because I was worried about you. I felt sure you were in danger, and I felt responsible."

Another harsh laugh. "Well, as you can see, you had no need to worry. I told you before that I know what I'm about. Now you've come in here with your damned sense of responsibility and complicated everything."

"Is that what you think?" David replied. "It seems to me

I've come just in time to stop you killing him—that's not what you came here to do, is it?"

"What do you mean?" Euan replied, his frowning gaze on Hugh. "I always meant to kill him. How could you have thought otherwise?"

David gaped at him. "You said you wanted to confront him," he said at last.

Euan smiled grimly. "And here we are. Confronting one another in the simplest way possible." A flickering glance at David. "Your trouble is you judge everyone else by your own standards, Davy. Most people aren't as good or honourable as you imagine."

"That's not true," David said. "*You* are a good man, Euan. A loving brother, a fine student, a loyal friend. You are not a man who murders for revenge. Please don't stain your soul with this crime."

Euan made a noise somewhere between despair and amusement. "You want me to let this cur live? Let him marry that stuck-up Galbraith whore and have a nice, comfortable life while Peter is sent across the sea in chains?"

Hugh made an angry noise and began to rise. "How dare you speak of Miss Gal—"

Euan interrupted this protest with an angry roar. "Shut your *fucking* mouth!" His gun arm stiffened, the pistol in his hand dark and deadly. His eyes blazed, and his thin, wiry body vibrated with tension. David twitched with the need to move, to intervene, but Balfour's hand on his left shoulder exerted pressure, keeping him in place.

"Think carefully," Balfour said, addressing Euan. His voice was calm and firm. "You've only got one shot. After that, you will be unarmed, and we will overcome you. You'll be arrested. Hanged. All this will have been for nothing. All you have to do to avoid that is to put down your gun and leave."

Euan considered that. "It wouldn't be for nothing," he

said at last, his gaze never wavering from the kneeling man. "*He* would be dead."

"And so would you be, soon enough."

Euan just shrugged, and David's heart wrenched to see how little the lad seemed to value his own life.

"If you lower your pistol," Balfour continued, his voice calm and low, "you can walk away. We won't stop you. Think of that." Balfour's intent black gaze was concentrated on the other man, and as his attention narrowed and deepened, so too did his grip of David's shoulder loosen, till his big hand was merely resting there.

David saw that Balfour believed he could persuade Euan. He didn't seem to have realised yet, as David had, that Euan's desire to revenge his brother was far stronger than his desire to save himself.

Balfour didn't know how little Euan had to live for.

But David knew—and more, that the only way to stop Euan's bullet from hitting Hugh was to put something else in the way.

Balfour's attention was all on Euan now. It only took a shrug to displace the heavy hand from David's shoulder and move smoothly in front of the kneeling man.

"*David!*"

He didn't miss the shock and fear in Balfour's voice. Nor the unfamiliar use of his own Christian name. He didn't turn, though. He didn't dare look away from the man in front of him.

"Get out of the way, Davy," Euan said, his voice soft and dangerous.

"Do as he says!" Balfour added forcefully.

David ignored Balfour, his gaze fixed on Euan. "I can't," he said. He wondered if either of them realised how serious he was. "I caused this. And I won't have a man's death on my conscience."

Euan's arm stayed where it was, the barrel of the pistol

pointing at David now. "I don't want to shoot you. You've been a good friend to me, till now."

David gave a tremulous smile, afraid despite his best efforts. "Then don't. Don't shoot me. Just do as Balfour said and leave. We won't stop you."

"You don't understand," Euan continued. "I can't allow you to stand in my way."

David shook his head. "No, *you* don't understand. It's like Balfour said—you've only got one shot. You leave now or you shoot me, but you're not getting Lees."

"David—" Balfour's voice was hoarse. "For Christ's sake, step away!"

Euan's eyes blazed. "Listen to him. Stand aside. Don't make me hurt you."

Without shifting his gaze from Euan, David slowly raised the knife Balfour had given him and tossed it away. It skittered across the floor to the other side of the room. David raised his other hand then, both palms facing outwards.

"I'm not making you do anything," he said, his voice trembling. "It's your choice whether to shoot me. But I won't be moving aside. I can't."

Euan's gaze shifted over David's shoulder to the man behind him. He looked despairing and angry. At the very end of his rope.

"I'll never forgive you for this," he whispered. "This was my only chance."

For a moment, David thought the lad was going to do it, that he was going to fire the bullet into David's body. He imagined the impact of it, caving his chest in, shattering bones, burning through flesh, and he began to tremble.

Euan's hand on the pistol stayed steady, his body the very picture of certainty and action. His face, though, told a more complex story. Grief was there, and hatred for the man who knelt behind David—and hesitancy.

When at last he spoke again, his voice was devoid of expression. "Come here, then."

"David, don't." Balfour's voice was firm, commanding.

David ignored him. "Cover Hugh," he said shortly and walked forward, his hands still raised.

A few paces brought him close enough to Euan that another inch would have the barrel of the gun pressing into his chest.

"Turn round."

David obeyed, noting with relief that Balfour had done as David had asked. He stood in front of Hugh now, his own pistol trained on Euan and David. He looked angry, his eyes flashing dark fire at David, his lips pressed tightly together.

An arm snaked round David's shoulders and pulled him back against Euan's chest. He could feel the prickle of the other man's beard growth at his ear.

"I believe you mean what you say about letting me go," Euan murmured, pressing the pistol against David's temple, "but I don't trust your friend there. So I need to keep you with me for now. We're going to walk backwards to the door."

David nodded, and they began to pace awkwardly backwards.

"You two," Euan said, raising his voice as they drew close to the doorway. "Stay exactly where you are. If you move so much as an inch, I'll put a bullet in his head."

Balfour and Hugh both nodded. Balfour wore a grim, unhappy look.

David heard the door creaking open behind him, felt the tension in Euan's arm drawing him back and the steely press of the pistol against the side of his head. His heart thudded as he watched Balfour and Hugh, praying neither of them would do anything rash or alarming.

As Euan pulled him through the doorway, Balfour's fists

clenched by his side. "Where are you taking him?" he demanded.

"Davy's coming with me for a little. He'll be back soon enough, provided you two don't move. And I'll hear you if you do. The floorboards creak something terrible."

Balfour gave another jerky nod, and the next moment, they were out and the door was swinging closed behind them, the torn-out, useless lock clattering against the frame.

Euan grabbed David's arm and turned him round, shoving him forward so roughly he stumbled. While David was righting his footing, the other man got behind him, pushing the barrel of his pistol in David's back.

"Come on," he grated. "Move!"

He hustled David down the corridor and the first two rickety flights of stairs. At the next landing, he grabbed David by the shoulder.

"This is where we part," he said. He looked at David for a long moment before adding fiercely, "I don't think you realise how close I came to killing you tonight."

"I do," David said. "But I had faith in you too."

Euan gave a harsh laugh. "You always see the best in people, Davy. I'm not sure if it's a weakness or a strength."

"I'm not as naïve as you think." David fished in his coat and pulled out a purse of coins—it was all the money he had. He pressed it into Euan's hands. "Here. Get out of the city. Don't look back. Forget Lees."

Euan gave him a long look, pocketing the purse. "I can't promise to do that. But I promise this. I'll pay you back one day." Then he was gone, his boot heels ringing out as he raced down the last flight of stairs.

David stayed where he was, gazing down the stairwell at the lad's diminishing figure. He waited till he heard the front door of the hotel being wrenched open, the decisive clang as it closed.

Then he counted to a hundred, slowly, to let Euan get well and truly away.

As he stood there, counting, the single candle that lit the stairwell landing guttered out. The flame died first; then, after a moment, a thin thread of smoke rose from its waxy grave and began to drift upwards.

David turned and followed it up to the third floor.

CHAPTER SIXTEEN

Balfour handed David a generous glass of whisky. They were in the drawing room of his townhouse, David perched stiffly on a brocade sofa. Hugh had been sent off to a bedchamber with a footman as his guide as soon as they arrived. Balfour had spoken not a word to his cousin in the carriage on the way here, his gaze averted as though he couldn't bring himself to look at the other man. He'd been quiet with David too, but not in the same way. His manner with David had been kind and concerned. Watchful.

"I should be getting home," David said, though he accepted the whisky and took a deep swallow, relishing the burn of the liquor.

Balfour regarded him silently, his expression faintly troubled.

"What is it?" David asked.

Balfour seemed reluctant to speak but eventually, when David kept looking at him questioningly, he muttered, "I'd rather you didn't."

"I beg your pardon?"

Balfour huffed in an exasperated way and strode over to the fireplace. The fire was burning merrily in the grate, but

Balfour grabbed the poker and went at the logs as though it needed stirring. When he finally straightened, he turned and said, "What if Euan MacLennan turns up at your rooms tonight?"

David was stunned into momentary silence. He thought of that big, warm hand on his shoulder. And Balfour calling out *"David!"* when he ran in front of Euan's pistol, even though Balfour always called him Lauriston. An odd, unfamiliar warmth grew in his belly.

"He won't," David said at last, adopting a deliberately light tone. "But your cousin had better keep an eye out, I'd say."

Balfour ignored that. "Why don't you stay here tonight? Not with me—my staff will make you up a chamber."

"There's no need—"

"Humour me," Balfour interrupted. "You seem to have a habit of running into trouble. Last time you were here, you managed to get attacked on the way home."

David felt himself flush, thinking of that night. Abruptly, he decided to give way. He was exhausted after all. "All right," he said, shrugging. "If you wish."

"Good," Balfour said, throwing himself into a chair and swallowing half the contents of his own glass. "What do you think MacLennan will do now?"

David considered. "His brother was transported a few weeks ago. They probably won't see each other ever again. Euan is desolate. And angry." He paused. "He may try to find your cousin again. I don't know."

Balfour brooded over that, staring into the fire.

David watched him. What a profile the man had. Like some ancient Roman general with his dark hair cut Brutus style and his strong, blunt features. A hint of aggression in that discontented jaw.

"May I make a request?" David said.

Balfour turned his head, eyes hooded. "It depends what it is," he growled.

Shamefully, excitement stirred in David at the promise in the other man's deep voice before he thrust that thought aside. He had a real favour to ask. Something he suspected Balfour would not be eager to agree.

"Don't pursue Euan."

A small shift in Balfour's expression and the hint of promise turned to caution. "You said yourself you think he'll go after Hugh again."

"And Hugh knows about him now. He can take care of himself. It's between them."

"I might despise him, but he's my cousin."

"And Euan is my friend. A friend I betrayed to save your cousin."

"And what if he succeeds next time, when I might have stopped him?"

"What if you stop him when he was never going to do anything?"

"Why should Hugh take that chance?"

David shook his head angrily. "Hugh? A man who lied to and betrayed innocent men, you mean? He *caused* this."

Balfour stayed silent, watching David carefully. "Do you fancy yourself in love with MacLennan?" he said at last.

"What? No!" He wasn't sure whether Balfour believed him or not. The man's gaze never wavered from his.

"The reason I am here, in Scotland," Balfour said eventually, "is because my aunt begged me to find Hugh. I promised I would try to extricate him from whatever my father had got him into. I have to keep that promise."

"And you have kept it. If you want to protect him further, there are other things you can do for him than go after Euan. Send him abroad. Give him a new name."

"That kind of help will take him away from Bella Galbraith."

"Maybe."

Balfour sighed. "If I send Hugh away now, he will think I want Bella for myself."

"And do you?" The words were out before David could stop them. He hated the smile they elicited from that beautifully carved mouth.

"She *would* make an ideal wife."

Goaded, David said waspishly, "Putting aside the fact she dislikes you, you mean?"

Balfour laughed, eyes crinkling at the corners. "How catty of you! I didn't think you'd stoop so low."

God, but he was handsome when he laughed. David felt a queer ache in his stomach that was only partly desire.

"I'm not being catty," David said. "It's merely an observation."

Balfour grinned. "You're right of course. Bella thinks it's her right to be worshipped, and she hates that I tease her mercilessly. Also, she has no sense of humour whatsoever."

Yes, that fitted.

"So," David said. "Do you agree to leave Euan alone?"

Balfour's smile died. David thought he was going to refuse. But when Balfour finally spoke, he surprised him. "All right. I'll leave MacLennan alone, and I'll find some way to put Hugh out of his reach. Does that satisfy you?"

"Yes, it does. Thank you." The words were heartfelt. He wondered if Balfour realised how much.

They fell into silence, the sound of the ticking clock on the mantel the only noise in the room. It might have been uncomfortable with someone else. Not with Balfour, though.

"Can I ask *you* something now?" Balfour said, breaking the silence.

"Of course."

"Why do you call me Balfour instead of Lord Murdo?"

David flushed. "I know it's not proper, but it's how I think of you," he admitted. When Balfour arched a brow, he continued, half reluctantly. "When we first met—that night in Stirling—you didn't disclose your title. You told me your name was Mr. Balfour, so from then on, that's how I thought of you. As Balfour. Even though I later learned you were the son of a marquess."

Balfour fixed his dark eyes on David. "You never thought of me as Murdo? You know that is my Christian name." His eyes were almost black, the colour of coffee. In this light, you couldn't see where the deep brown of the iris met the pure black of the pupil.

David flushed, thrown by the odd intimacy of the question. "I can't say I have."

Balfour glanced away. "Odd, aren't they," he said after a pause. "Names, I mean."

"What do you mean?"

Balfour gave a funny little half-hitched smile. "The only person in the whole world who's ever called me Murdoch—my proper given name—is my mother. Neither my father nor any of my siblings call me anything but Murdo."

David couldn't help but smile. "You have a mother?" he teased lightly. "I thought you were made of marble."

Balfour offered a tight smile. "Had," he said. "She passed away."

David's smile faded. "I'm sorry—"

Balfour waved the apology away. "It was a long time ago."

"How many siblings do you have?" David asked. "I only have one, a brother, Drew."

"There are six of us," Balfour replied. "My oldest brother, Harris, then Iain, then me. And the three girls."

"It must be nice, to have such a large family."

"Sometimes. What does your mother call you?"

"Davy."

Balfour raised an eyebrow. "That's what MacLennan called you."

David shrugged. "That's different."

"How?"

"In ways you can't understand."

"Explain it to me."

"Oh, I'd need much more whisky for that." David's tone was light, teasing. But Balfour rose from his chair and fetched the decanter anyway, refilling David's glass with a slosh of amber fluid.

David sighed, resigned. He took a long swallow and leaned back in his chair. "Where I come from, most people use my given name."

"Where do you come from?"

"A village called Midlauder, about twenty miles from here. My father leases a small farm there. In Midlauder, there's the big house where the laird lives—his estate manager runs the home farm. Then there are the tenanted farms, like my father's. Most of the people who live in the village are labourers, other than Mr. Odell, the minister and Mr. Graeme, the physician. Then there's the smithy and the inn. And one shop, run by the widow McAndrew." He smiled a little wistfully. "It's a small place."

"Believe it or not," Balfour said drily, "I'm familiar with the concept of villages."

"Ah, but you would've been the son of the big house."

"Well, yes."

"What did they call you when you were a boy? Lord Murdo?"

"Most of them, yes. Or Master Murdo."

David smiled. "You're so used to it, you don't even notice. Men of your class—the way you're addressed—it tells the story of who you are and where you came from."

Balfour arched a brow. "But not men like you?"

"Not to the same degree. It's different. When I was boy, everyone called me Davy, except my father."

"What did he call you?"

"David. Always my Sunday name." He smiled, half fond, half sad. "My brother's Andrew, but he got Drew, even from my father. I was different."

"And now," Balfour said, "you're a man of letters, and they call you Mr. Lauriston. You've moved up in the world. Congratulations." He tipped his head back, emptying his glass.

"Not everyone. When I met the weavers and their families, I saw how I intimidated them—how we all did. So I told them I was just like them. I told them I didn't come from money, and I told them about the wee farm my family lived on and how hard it was to make ends meet. I told them my name was Davy. And so that was what they called me."

Balfour turned his head during that speech, and when David finished, their eyes met and held.

"That's why Euan calls me Davy. And why I call him Euan. Because we're the same, in a way."

"In more ways than one. He's a university man like yourself, isn't he?"

"You know about that?"

"Hugh mentioned it earlier. He thinks—like my father—that educating working men is a dangerous thing."

"Do you think that?"

Balfour shrugged. "Too late to worry about it. The world is changing. My father is trying to preserve a world of aristocratic power and privilege that's already dead. He doesn't see it, but I do."

"Doesn't seem like it's dead to me," David said.

"No. Well, there's nothing like a dying animal for fighting back, is there? But you only have to look at the aristocracy to see we've only got a generation or two left in us. All we've got is land—and most of us are selling that off to pay our gambling debts. We don't make anything; we don't even manage what we do have very well, most of us."

"You aren't you going to fight for it?" David asked, curious.

Balfour yawned and shook his head, stretching his legs out before him. "I don't see the point of fighting losing battles for other people. I'd rather concentrate on making the best of what I've got in the here and now."

"Just because you lose a battle, doesn't mean it was never worth fighting."

"A noble sentiment, Lauriston. How very you."

David bristled, hating the fact that Balfour's mocking words made him feel like a naïve boy. "There's nothing wrong with noble sentiments."

"No," Balfour agreed. "But they won't keep you warm at night."

"You're not without principles," David said. "You came all this way to save your cousin, didn't you?"

"That's different," Balfour said, shrugging. "I owed my aunt a debt. She did something for me a long time ago. Besides, Hugh is family."

"You value your family, then, at least."

Balfour laughed. "Don't try to find a virtue in me, Lauriston. You won't. Family is just another kind of privilege. Little groups of people, sticking together to further their shared interests. I'm not averse to making such allegiances to advance myself."

"That's not all family is," David protested, thinking of his hard-working father, his brusque, loving mother, kindly, warm-hearted Drew. The fierce and helpless love he felt for them all, despite everything.

"No? In my experience it is."

"Then I pity you."

"Don't waste your time, I'm perfectly content."

They were such opposites, David thought. Different in every possible way.

Suddenly, he felt overwhelmingly tired.

He set his glass down on the occasional table next to the sofa and stood.

"You know, I think I'll go home after all," he said.

Balfour looked up at him, a moment's disappointment in his dark gaze before he masked it. "You're not staying the night?"

"No," David replied. "I've decided I need my own bed."

Balfour's gaze moved over him, and David felt unsettled, standing while the other man examined him with that bland expression. What was he thinking? At last, Balfour levered himself up from his chair. "If you insist," he said at last. "I'll call for my carriage to take you."

"There's no need."

"Don't argue." Balfour sighed. "Please."

He crossed to the room and pulled the bell rope.

"I'll be going back to London tomorrow," Balfour added in a flat voice. "So this is good-bye."

"Good-bye?" David wished he could bite back the word as soon as it was out. It seemed to him his voice rang with disappointment.

"I don't expect I'll be in Scotland again for a while."

"I see. Well, I'll wish you all the best, then." David thrust out his hand.

For a moment, Balfour simply stared at his outstretched hand, till David felt so uncomfortable he wanted to draw it back. But then Balfour took it, and in one swift movement, turned David's hand over, palm down, and lowered his head to press a kiss to the back of it.

Balfour's lips were soft and warm, but the fingers holding David's hand were strong and determined. The gesture made David feel supremely off-balance. It was typically Balfour: challenging and humorous at once. Making a woman of David with his queer courtliness. It was...romantic.

David pulled his hand back swiftly, masking how shaken he was with a laugh.

"I'm glad I met you, Lauriston," Balfour said, his expression back to the usual careless amusement. "You've made these last weeks very interesting."

"Well, I'm glad to have entertained you," David countered, adopting a determinedly light tone.

"Are you? You certainly have, whether you intended to or not." He gave a wry smile. "Are you quite sure you won't stay the night?"

For a moment, David hesitated, but he knew it would be a mistake. An intimacy had sprung up between them tonight—not the physical kind, a different sort—that unsettled him in ways he couldn't put a name to. "Yes, thank you," he said at last. "I'm quite sure."

Was that regret in Balfour's gaze? If so, it was good-humoured enough. "Very well."

The footman came then, and Balfour went to confer with him, giving him his orders. When the footman had gone, he strolled over to David, who had risen from his chair.

"Will you permit me to give you one bit of advice, before we say farewell?"

Wary, David nodded.

"Don't rule out marrying Elizabeth Chalmers. She's in love with you, and she'd be a good wife to you. She could give you children and make you a home."

It was so close to David's own recent thoughts on the matter that he almost laughed. Instead he merely shook his head. "I couldn't do that to her," he said. "She deserves a husband who will love her fully."

Balfour's lips thinned, and his eyes glittered. All at once, his good humour was gone.

"There you go again," he snapped. "Always the bloody martyr, aren't you? With your terrible affliction that you won't subject any innocent souls to? Christ, why don't you just let yourself have a bit of happiness? Marry a woman who loves you and slake your needs with men on occasion.

It's not as though thousands of others don't do it every day!"

"Is that what you're going to do?"

"Yes! Yes, it is! I don't want to be like you. I want everything this damned world has to offer! If that means bending the truth a little here and there, what's the harm? Christ, you're so damnably yes-or-no about everything! So judgmental—"

"I'm not judging you," David protested. "I couldn't give a damn what you do—but I *can't be* what I am not. I can't, and that's the beginning and the end of it."

"Christ almighty, don't you want to be *happy*?"

David knew, somehow, that that was a cry from the heart. He looked at Balfour, and it was as though the man was standing naked before him. The always present amusement had been wiped away entirely, and on his face was an expression of naked longing. It made David wonder what it was that Balfour longed for that made him look like that.

"I'm not sure life is about being happy," David answered with quiet honesty.

Balfour gave a harsh laugh at that. "Another Lauristonian sentiment," he sneered. "I should have predicted that one. Tell me, then. If life isn't about pleasure or happiness, what is it about? Tell me, Lauriston, so I can learn from your great wisdom."

It was tempting to say nothing, to walk away. He knew Balfour would mock whatever answer he gave. But for some reason, he felt compelled to utter it.

"I think it's about being true to yourself," he said at length.

He was right—Balfour laughed. It was an ugly sound. A sneering, mocking insult. "To thine own self be true? Christ, that's rich, coming from you! You hate your own guts because you like cock, that's how true to yourself *you* are!"

David felt a lump rise in his throat and had to swallow

against it. He couldn't deny that accusation. He thought of the night he'd lain in Balfour's bed while the man kissed and stroked and suckled him. He thought of the wave of unprecedented tenderness that had washed over him afterwards.

Balfour wasn't finished yet.

"You deny the very essence of who you are, and you do it every single fucking day. And then you have the gall to turn around and tell me that if I have the temerity to want the things that other men take for granted, I'm not being *true* to myself?"

"I never said that," David replied. "If you decide to marry, that's a matter for you and your conscience. For my part, I won't do it. Yes, I hate what I am at times, but at least I accept myself enough to realise that I can't lie my way through life, pretending to prefer women when I don't."

At that moment, there was a knock on the door, and Balfour, who had opened his mouth to speak, swallowed his words and barked, "Enter!"

It was Johnston the footman. He'd brought David's hat and coat—freshly brushed—along with the news that the carriage was waiting. If he'd overhead any of their argument, he gave no sign. Balfour dismissed him impatiently.

David shrugged the coat on and jammed his hat on his head. Suddenly he felt regretful and empty. This was likely the last time he'd see Balfour and, for some reason, that thought left David with a yawning chasm inside him.

"Believe it or not," he said gravely, looking squarely at the other man, "I wish you every happiness." He went to walk past Balfour and was surprised when the other man caught his upper arm in a strong grip. Before he could protest, Balfour took David's face in his big, warm hands and kissed him fiercely.

It was a painful, desperate kiss. Balfour's hard mouth ground the soft tissue behind David's lips against his teeth and he made a strange, almost animal noise in his chest.

Before David could even react, Balfour had thrust him away, and they stood staring at one another, panting. "Don't wish me happiness, damn you," he said bitterly.

David raised his fingers to his lips, and they came away bloody. He stared at the crimson smears on his fingertips for a long moment, aching for he didn't know what.

"You should go," Balfour muttered, turning away. "The carriage is waiting."

CHAPTER SEVENTEEN

Three months later

"Your turn, Davy," his mother said, and shoved the bundled-up bairn into his arms.

David startled, making the rest of the small assembled group laugh. He fumbled for a moment before relaxing his arm, creating a secure curve for Drew and Letty's firstborn, his nephew, Allan David Lauriston.

The baby stared up at him, winsome and oddly grave. His eyes were an extraordinary dark blue, the gold-tipped lashes surprisingly long. He looked absurdly new, this tiny person. Absurdly delicate. The tender folds of his little eyelids made some wall inside David crumble away. The feeling made his eyes smart with hot tears. He disguised them with his bent head, waiting until the unfamiliar burst of emotion had passed before he looked up again.

Everyone was watching him. His mother and father, Drew and Letty. His mother looked fond, Drew and Letty proud, their eyes on the babe. His father seemed sad.

"He's a bonny lad," David said, addressing the remark to

Letty, who kissed him on the cheek before retrieving the baby. She couldn't keep her hands off him, David's mother had complained. A typical new mother, she sniffed, but David could tell she wasn't really annoyed. The truth was, no one could keep their hands off the baby. They'd been fighting good-naturedly over him all day. Even David's father, who had dandled him too roughly, as though he was a toddler of two instead of a newborn babe.

They gathered round him again now, debating whether to feed him or put him down to sleep, all except David and his father, who looked at David and said, "Come and have a walk with me, lad."

David nodded. They both rose and went into the kitchen, shoving on boots and coats before walking out into the cold January day.

"This way," his father said, setting off for the path to the north field.

For a while, they walked in silence. David's father wasn't a great talker. He only spoke when he had something to say. David suspected this might be one of those rare occasions.

It was a miserable day with a heavy, grey sky. The bitter winter wind did nothing to dry out the freezing damp that clung to every tree and rock and every inch of the hard ground. Last week's drifts of white snow had melted for the most part, leaving only dirty banks of white-and-brown crust on either side of the steep dirt path that led up to the north field. They trudged up, hands deep in their pockets, heads lowered against the wind.

When they got to the top of the hill, David's father took off his cap and leaned on the wooden gate of the north field, staring out at the valley below them. It was good farming here. Fertile ground and mostly flat with decent soil. Not exactly the most romantic landscape, but a man could make a living here. David joined his father at the gate, resting one booted foot on the lowest rung and leaning his forearms on the topmost one. The familiarity of the gesture made him feel nostalgic, remembering a time when he wasn't tall enough to see over this old gate.

"You could have what Drew's got," his father said, eyes still looking straight ahead. "A wife and bairns. You'd be a good father, David."

The warm nostalgia dissipated. David paused before replying. "I dearly wish I could, Dad. But I can't."

His father's posture didn't alter, and after a few moments, he nodded, as though David's words were no surprise at all. His profile was craggy, the short brush of his salt-and-pepper hair blown back by the biting January wind. "You've chosen a hard road," he said.

"I wouldn't call it a choice," David replied.

"There's always choices. And you always seem to pick the toughest ones." The old man stuck his cap back on, his mouth twisting into a smile of sorts. "You could've taken the apprentice position with Adam Jamieson and got a good trade. But instead you did all that learning with Mr. Odell, and off to university you went to become a fancy lawyer."

"You encouraged me," David pointed out, smiling. It was true. His father had groused, but he'd scrimped and saved to help pay David's tuition. The old man valued education above everything.

"I knew once you set your mind to it you'd be sure to do it. That's always how you were. Like when you took that whipping for Drew for leaving this very gate open and letting my best ram out."

"I couldn't sit down for a week." David grinned.

"And when I caught you with William Lennox."

David's grin died on his face. "Dad—"

The old man's face was grim, the deep lines at the corners of his eyes, from all those years outdoors, showing his age. He stared straight ahead. "God help me, David, I *wanted* you to lie to me that day. I wanted to believe it was anything but what my eyes told me."

David's chest felt tight. "I know," he said thickly. "I'm so sorry."

"But you wouldn't deny it."

"I...couldn't. I—"

"Even though he denied it fast enough."

Christ.

Like a knife in his gut, the memory of that betrayal pierced David all over again. William saying it was a mistake. That David had pushed him; that he'd allowed himself to be persuaded into the embrace despite his unwillingness. David shook his head at the wintry valley in helpless denial.

"How can I be proud of you for *that*?" his father said sadly, shifting his whole body to look at David. David turned his head to meet the old man's stony gaze. "And how can I not?" he added.

The pain in his father's eyes wasn't to be borne.

"I'm so sorry," he said again, wretchedly.

"You know what, Davy?"

"What?"

"William Lennox—Sir William, as he is now—has married a fine English lady, and they have a wee lassie. Another babe coming, so I hear."

"Is that so?" David tried to imagine William with a daughter of his own. Would she have the same green-gold eyes as her father? The same dark hair? Or would she look like her mother?

"Aye, it's so. He's not got your scruples, lad." The old man sighed. "But like I said, you never did take the easy road. It makes me want to weep for you sometimes."

David didn't know what to say to that, so he said nothing and the old man turned back to look out over the valley.

After a while, his father said, "I never told your mother.

After, I mean. I didn't want her worrying about you going to hell."

David swallowed, guilt swamping him. "Thank you," he muttered.

"And I've thought about it a lot since then. I reckon it's no sin, Davy, if you don't act on it. God sends strange things to try us. Sometimes they seem awful unfair. Look at Job. But we cannot know His purpose for us. All we can do is submit ourselves to His will and do what is right."

David said nothing to that. He couldn't. When he swallowed against the hot lump of grief trapped in his throat, it felt like swallowing a piece of his own heart. It was a monumental struggle to bring himself under control and avoid the final shame of giving way to tears.

It seemed, though, that the old man had said all he wanted to say. After that last pronouncement, he fell silent. Now he stared straight ahead, eyes narrowed, as though an answer might be out there, somewhere. A clue that might explain the whimsies of his God.

"It's cold, Dad," David said after a little while. "Shall we go back?"

"You go," his father said without turning his head. "I'm going to bide here a wee bit. I'll come back by and by."

He left his father looking over the land he'd farmed his whole life, and trudged back down the hill. Four o'clock, and already it was getting dark. Damn, but these winter days were short.

So William was married, and with children no less. It was hardly a surprise, David supposed.

For some reason, though, the news made him think of Murdo Balfour, of all people. Balfour, whom he'd somehow managed to shove to the back of his mind and not think of for weeks now. He hadn't seen the man since the night they'd seen off Euan MacLennan. Presumably he was back in London. David knew he'd probably never see him again. It was entirely pointless to waste time wondering about him. But wonder he did.

Angry with himself, David punished himself by imagining the man with Isabella Galbraith, even though he knew she probably wouldn't be his choice now. It would be someone like her, though. Someone beautiful and accomplished. He imagined Balfour kissing her. Balfour burying himself between her soft white thighs. He imagined them with a clutch of dark-haired children. They'd have beautiful children.

And then he thought of Balfour's eyes glittering with lust, his hand wrapped round his cock as he stared down at David's prone, sated body.

He thought of Balfour touching him, more intimately than anyone had before, or probably would again.

"You're beautiful."

Christ Jesus.

That night—that moment—had been the sweetest of all David's life. And if thinking that made him wicked and bound for hell, he wasn't sure he had it in him to repent. But Christ, it was bittersweet. More bitter than sweet, truth to tell. Sweet to know that for once in his life, he'd known such tenderness, but oh so bitter to know it would never come again.

For one awful moment, all David's darkness rose in him: misery, loneliness, envy. It blazed through him like an inferno in his blood. It roared through him and immolated him and left him like a husk. He opened his eyes and realised he was bent over, one arm braced on his thigh, his throat thick with unshed tears.

Then the pain ebbed, and he straightened. He wrapped all those thoughts up in black crepe and moved them to the back of his mind. He forbade himself to think about them anymore.

He took a deep breath and set off down the path again,

and when he came round the bend, it was to see the farm-house, with candles glowing in the windows, like a light-house calling him to safety.

When he opened the door, the savoury aroma of beef stew and dumplings assailed him, and his brother called him over to the fire to play a game of dominoes. His father came in a little later, and it seemed he was back to normal again. He joined his sons and accepted a cup of ale from Letty.

They ate a good dinner. Afterwards, David's father broke open the rarely broached whisky, and the three men settled down to a more earnest game of dominoes while his mother sewed and Letty crooned to the baby.

When the game ended, David stood and went over to his sister-in-law.

"May I sit with you, Letty?"

She smiled. "Of course. Do you want to hold Allan again?"

"All right."

She shifted up, making room for him, then carefully lifted the sleeping baby and placed him in David's arms.

He was a warm wee weight, the shape of his little body just made to sit in the crook of an arm. His extravagant lashes kissed cheeks that looked like apricots in the fire's glow. Like a little prince, he lay, confident of his welcome, helplessly trusting and full of potential.

Would this child be a farmer, like his father and grandfa-ther before him, or would he want to seek out another path, as his uncle had done? Perhaps one day, he would need David's help. It was a thought that warmed David unex-pectedly.

David might never have a wife and children of his own, but he had a family, and more besides. Good health, friends, work that brought him great satisfaction.

And besides all that, he'd tasted, if only once in his life, real, honest passion.

With Murdo Balfour.

How could he regret that? How could he regret the best, and sweetest moment of all his life?

He swallowed against the sudden lump in his throat and looked up to find his mother smiling at him. His father and Drew bent over their game. Letty dozing beside him, an exhausted new mother. The baby in his arms.

This house was full of love. And it was enough.

For now, it was enough.

The End

THANK YOU, DEAR READER

Thank you for reading this book.
Thank you for spending your valuable time with
David and Murdo. I hope you enjoyed their company. I
realise I've left them in a difficult place here, but their story
continues in books 2 and 3 in the trilogy, and I hope you will
agree the journey is worth it.

I love hearing from my readers. You can:

~ Email me at authorjoannachambers@gmail.com
~ Visit my website at www.joannachambers.com
~ Connect with me on social media through those
cute little icons below.
~ Sign up for my newsletter at my website for up to date
information about my books, freebies and special deals.

If you have time, I'd be very grateful if you'd consider leaving
a review on an online review site. Reviews are so helpful for
book visibility and I appreciate every one.

Joanna Chambers

BEGUILED (ENLIGHTENMENT #2)

Beguiled

Two years after his last encounter with cynical nobleman Lord Murdo Balfour, David Lauriston accidentally meets him again in the heart of Edinburgh.

King George IV is about to make his first visit to Edinburgh and Murdo has been sent North by his politician father to represent his aristocratic family at the celebrations.

David and Murdo's last parting was painful—and on Murdo's part, bitter—but Murdo's feelings seem to have mellowed in the intervening years. So much so, that he suggests to David that they enjoy each other's company during Murdo's stay in the capital.

Despite his initial reservations, David cannot put Murdo's proposal from his mind, and soon find himself at Murdo's door—and in his arms.

But other figures from David's past are converging on the city, and as the pomp and ceremony of the King's visit unfolds around them, David is drawn into a chain of events that will threaten everything: his career, his wellbeing, and the fragile bond that, despite David's best intentions, is growing between him and Murdo.

READ ON FOR A TASTER OF BEGUILED...

It wanted ten minutes till five o'clock when David reached the tailor's. He was on time, thankfully, if only just. But when he pushed at the door, he found it locked.

Frowning, he rang the bell. When there was no answer, he rang it again, pulling the rope several times, but still no one came. Stepping away from the door, he went to the window and peered in through one of the small, thick panes. The shop was gloomy, but he saw the dim outline of a figure moving around.

"Hello there!" he called, rapping sharply at the glass. "Let me in, will you? I've a fitting arranged."

The figure moved forward into the light, and David could see now that it was a young lad, the tailor's assistant, presumably. A few steps from the door, he froze and looked over his shoulder towards the back of the shop, then glanced back at David and gave a helpless shrug.

Angry now, David rapped at the glass again. "I've an appointment!" he cried. "You can check—the name's David Lauriston. Mr. Riddell knows all about it."

The boy gave another shrug, his expression apologetic, then scuttled off. Was he going to see Mr. Riddell? Or was he just escaping?

Damn. David hadn't a hope of getting a suit made to Sir Walter's ridiculous specifications if Mr. Riddell didn't see him today.

He rapped the door sharply with his knuckles and rang the bell again, but after several minutes of this, it was beginning to look hopeless. Furious, he turned from the door, ready to stalk off, when the scrape of a key in the lock made him turn back.

The door opened, and a boy's anxious face poked out. "Mr. Lauriston?"

David stepped forward. "Yes."

"You're to come in, sir, please." The boy opened the door a little more, though not by much, as though he feared a multitude might storm the gates.

With an exasperated sigh, David stepped past him, frowning to find the shop floor empty.

"Where is Mr. Riddell?"

"He's in the back, sir," the boy whispered, "with a customer. A lord, sir!"

A lord. A peer who had sailed in and stolen David's appointment.

"Is that why the door was locked?" he demanded, frowning.

"Yes, sir. He came an hour ago wanting to order new clothes, so Mr. Riddell bade me lock up and turn anyone else away."

"Despite their appointments?"

The lad nodded and eyed the back shop nervously. "Aye, but when you kept knocking, I went back and told Mr. Riddell you wouldn't go, and the lordship, he said to let you in if you have an appointment."

"So I have the man who stole my appointment to thank for it being kept after all?" David didn't know whether to resent the man or not. "I certainly don't have your master to thank for it, do I?"

"I shouldn't have told you," the boy said, flushing. "Mr. Riddell always says I prattle on too much." He swallowed, perhaps contemplating the scold he'd get for his loose tongue.

David sighed. "I won't say anything—so long as Mr. Riddell honours my appointment, I don't much care. But I need this new suit before the King comes."

The boy sagged with relief. "Thank you, sir. May I trouble you to take your coat off, then? Mr. Riddell asked me to start taking your measurements."

"Very well," David said and took a step towards the back shop.

"No!" the lad protested, colouring again when David turned to look at him in surprise. "There's only one room back there, and Mr. Riddell's seeing to his lordship in there. We'll have to do it here."

"In the front shop?" David said disbelieving. "Where anyone might walk in?"

"The door's locked, sir, and you only need take your coat and boots off, if you please."

"Very well." David sighed impatiently, lifting his hands to unbutton his coat.

Flashing a grateful smile, the lad scuttled off to find his measuring tape and notebook. Soon he was taking every conceivable measurement of David's body: the length of each arm, its circumference in three separate places, the breadth of his shoulders, the line that ran from his armpit to his waist. The lad had just dropped to his knees to measure David's inside leg, when the rumble of low voices, then footsteps, signalled that Mr. Riddell and his aristocratic customer had completed their business and were about to come into the front shop.

Although he was very far from undressed, David felt exposed standing in the middle of the front shop, being measured in his stockinged feet. He looked over his shoulder in the direction of the approaching men, readying himself to say something. A quip to disguise his discomfort, and perhaps to make his displeasure known: *Please excuse my state of undress; it is so difficult to find a tailor at the moment, a man has to take what he can get. Unless he is a peer, of course...*

Mr. Riddell was the first to emerge through the connecting door—short, stocky and grey-headed, a measuring tape round his neck and the lapel of his coat glittering with pins. The other man was just behind him, and when he came through the doorway, he paused, his gaze raking the room till he found David. And smiled. A big, generous smile that dimpled one of his cheeks and made his dark eyes flash with infectious good humour.

Murdo Balfour.

"Mr. Lauriston." His smile deepened. "What a pleasant surprise!"

Only then did David realise that he had frozen and that his mouth was hanging open.

"Balfour—" he said.

He was almost surprised to hear his own voice uttering the name. Or rather breathing it, disbelieving. Rooted to the spot, he stared at the other man for long moments, his heart racing.

When they'd parted, two full years ago, Balfour had kissed David so angrily, David's lip had broken and bled.

"Don't wish me happiness, damn you..."

For days after, there had been a mark. When it was gone, David had almost missed it.

"I see you're being—measured up," Balfour said, interrupting David's swirling thoughts. He managed to make the ordinary observation sound almost indecent, and infuriatingly, David felt heat invade his cheeks.

ALSO BY JOANNA CHAMBERS

CAPITAL WOLVES DUET

Gentleman Wolf

Master Wolf

ENLIGHTENMENT SERIES

Provoked

Beguiled

Enlightened

Seasons Pass*

The Bequest*

Unnatural

Restored

* exclusive bonus stories for newsletter subscribers

WINTERBOURNE SERIES

Introducing Mr Winterbourne

Mr Winterbourne's Christmas

WITH ANNIKA MARTIN

Enemies Like You

PORTHKENNACK SERIES (RIPTIDE)

A Gathering Storm

Tribute Act

OTHER NOVELS

The Dream Alchemist

Unforgivable

Made in the USA
Monee, IL
20 May 2021